ALISSA AND THE DUNGEONS OF GRIMROCK
by Jillian Ross

Princess Alissa can't help worrying. Balin, her wizard friend and teacher, is long overdue from a trip.

Her worst fears prove true when Balin's parrot reappears and croaks out his message: "Captured!" There's no doubt in Alissa's mind that the parrot means Balin.

At once Alissa and her friend Lia set off in search of the wizard. Their journey leads them through a wild forest to the dark castle of Grimrock. The master of Grimrock is an evil sorcerer—and Balin's worst enemy.

Getting into the castle proves easy enough. It's getting out that concerns Alissa. She must manage to free Balin and escape before the sorcerer finds out exactly who she is.

Stardust Classics Series

Alissa

Alissa, Princess of Arcadia

A strange old wizard helps Alissa solve a mysterious riddle and save her kingdom.

Alissa and the Castle Ghost

The princess hunts a ghost as she tries to right a long-ago injustice.

Alissa and the Dungeons of Grimrock

Alissa must free her wizard friend, Balin, when he's captured by an evil sorcerer.

Laurel

Laurel the Woodfairy

Laurel sets off into the gloomy Great Forest to track a new friend—who may have stolen the woodfairies' most precious possession.

Laurel and the Lost Treasure

In the dangerous Deeps, Laurel and her friends join a secretive dwarf in a hunt for treasure.

Laurel Rescues the Pixies

Laurel tries to save her pixie friends from a forest fire that could destroy their entire village.

Kat

Kat the Time Explorer

Stranded in Victorian England, Kat tries to locate the inventor who can restore her time machine and send her home.

Kat and the Emperor's Gift

In the court of Kublai Khan, Kat comes to the aid of a Mongolian princess who's facing a fearful future.

Kat and the Secrets of the Nile

At an archaeological dig in Egypt of 1892, Kat uncovers a plot to steal historical treasures—and blame an innocent man.

Design and Art Direction by Vernon Thornblad

This book may be purchased in bulk at discounted rates for sales promotions, premiums, fundraising, or educational purposes. For more information, write the Special Sales Department at the address below or call 1-888-809-0608.

Just Pretend, Inc.
Attn: Special Sales Department
One Sundial Avenue, Suite 201
Manchester, NH 03103

Visit us online at www.justpretend.com

ALISSA
and the Dungeons of Grimrock

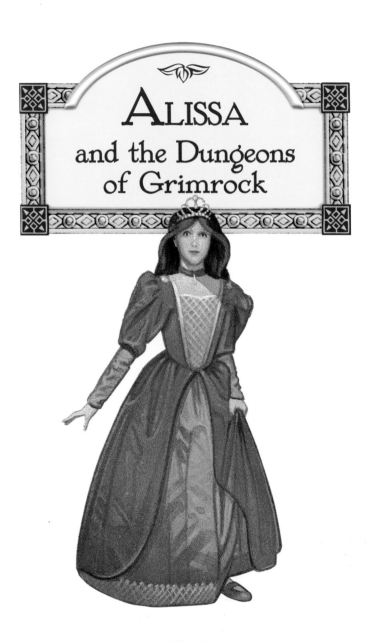

by Jillian Ross

Illustrations by Nick Backes
Cover Art by Patrick Faricy
Spot Illustrations by Katherine Salentine

Stardust
CLASSICS

Just Pretend, Inc.
Attn: Publishing Division
One Sundial Avenue, Suite 201
Manchester, NH 03103

Stardust Classics is a registered trademark
of Just Pretend, Inc.

First Edition
Printed in Hong Kong
04 03 02 01 00 99   10 9 8 7 6 5 4 3 2

Publisher's Cataloging-in-Publication
(Provided by Quality Books, Inc.)

Ross, Jillian.
    Alissa and the dungeons of Grimrock / by Jillian Ross; illustrations by Nick Backes; spot illustrations by Katherine Salentine. -- 1st ed.
    p. cm. -- (Stardust classics. Alissa; #3)

    SUMMARY: Princess Alissa must rescue her wizard friend Balin from the evil sorcerer who has imprisoned him in the dark castle of Grimrock.

    Preassigned LCCN: 98-65893
    ISBN: 1-889514-15-2 (hardcover)
    ISBN: 1-889514-16-0 (pbk.)

    1. Princesses--Juvenile fiction. 2. Wizards--Juvenile fiction.
    I. Backes, Nick. II. Salentine, Katherine. III. Title. IV. Series.

PZ7.R67Alc 1998   [Fic]
                                    QBI98-686

Contents

CHAPTER ONE

Captured!

lissa set down the picnic basket with a thud.

"I still say that Balin should have taken me along," she complained.

At the sound of Alissa's voice, a guard looked around. He was standing watch nearby, along the castle's outer wall.

"Alissa, shhh! He'll hear you," warned Lia.

"I wasn't that loud," protested Alissa. But Lia was right, so she lowered her voice.

It wouldn't do to have someone overhear her talking about Balin. For several months now, the wizard had been giving Alissa lessons in both wisdom and magic.

But those lessons—and Balin's presence in the kingdom—remained a secret. Other than Alissa, only a few people knew about the powerful old wizard. Lia, Alissa's best friend and lady-in-waiting, sometimes visited Balin's tower. And King Edmund, Alissa's father, had studied with the wizard as a boy.

Alissa went on, "I should be with Balin. After all, I *am* his student."

"You're also the princess," Lia pointed out.

Alissa sighed. "I know. And I know that means I have duties here. It's just that I wish..." She frowned before continuing. "I wish I knew what Balin was doing right now."

As they talked, the girls unpacked their picnic lunch. The

1

sight of food made Alissa willing to set aside her worries for a bit. She and Lia settled on the grass and ate.

For a while, Alissa studied the countryside. They had chosen the edge of the castle grounds for their picnic. It was a beautiful spot, even if it was a bit too peaceful for Alissa's taste. Nearby stood the two horses the girls had ridden. Beyond them stretched flower-filled meadows. Not far off, the castle's stone walls gleamed in the sunlight.

Lia's voice interrupted Alissa's thoughts. "At least you can practice your magic lessons while Balin is gone."

Alissa shook her head. "Right before he left, Balin started teaching me about reading the past from ashes. We didn't have time to get very far. So I can't do very much without his help."

She went on. "Besides, I miss him. I even miss crabby old Bartok." Balin's parrot had a habit of squawking "Begone!" at visitors— especially Alissa.

"You do have other lessons," observed Lia. "Embroidery, fine manners, linen folding..."

"Please don't remind me!" Alissa begged, rolling her eyes. "Why do my great-aunts insist I know all that?"

Lia's green eyes sparkled with laughter. It wasn't the first time she'd heard this complaint. Alissa's mother had died when she was a baby, and the princess had been raised by her father. King Edmund saw nothing strange about letting his daughter have the run of the kingdom. That meant that in her free time, Alissa had done as she pleased. She'd ridden with the pages, swum in the moat, and spent hours in the busy kitchen.

Things had changed once Alissa reached her tenth birthday. Her great-aunts decided it was time to take her under their wings. The princess—who would one day be queen—must become a proper lady.

Alissa picked at a spot on her skirt. "I don't think their lessons have helped me much anyway. See? I've managed to spill something, as usual. It's a good thing I'm not wearing one of my best dresses."

Alissa glanced at her friend. Lia looked as neat and clean as she had that morning. Sometimes Alissa thought that of the two of them, Lia might make a better princess.

But Lia wasn't the princess; Alissa was. She knew she must accept the bad things about that along with the good.

Now Alissa returned to the subject of the wizard. "What's really bothering me is that Balin has been gone so long," she said. "I keep checking the tower. Yet there's no sign of him."

"I know," agreed Lia. "And it's strange that he's made two trips in the past month. I thought he almost never left the kingdom."

Alissa's eyes narrowed. "I'm worried," she admitted.

She reached up to touch the locket at her neck. Deep in thought, she ran her fingers over the crescent moon on its surface. More than two weeks ago, Balin had placed the locket around her neck. He'd told her not to take it off until he said so. His face, half-hidden by his flowing white beard, had been wrinkled with concern. She'd begged to know where he was going and why. But Balin had refused to tell her.

"He told me he'd be back in a week," continued Alissa. "Balin never breaks a promise. I know he's in trouble."

"What did he tell you about his first trip?" asked Lia.

"He said an old friend had sent for him," answered the princess. "Someone who needed his help. But when Balin arrived at the meeting place, no one was there. He had no idea who had tricked him. Or why."

"That *is* strange," commented Lia. "Still, don't you think Balin can take care of himself? You know how powerful his magic is."

"Remember, he says magic can't do everything," replied Alissa. "Besides, there's something else."

"What?"

"A wooden box is missing from the tower," Alissa revealed. "I noticed right after Balin left for the second time. He kept this strange box on a shelf. There was a dragon carved on its lid."

"Maybe Balin took the box with him," Lia suggested. "Do you know what he keeps in it?"

"No. And I asked him about it more than once. All he'd tell me was that the box must never leave Arcadia. So why would he take it with him?"

Lia shrugged. "I don't understand either. Though if he did, I'm sure he had a good reason."

With that, Lia got to her feet. "It's time we got back to the castle."

"For more lessons," grumbled Alissa. She rose and began helping Lia pack up the basket.

Just as they finished packing, they heard a loud rustling of leaves overhead. Both girls jumped when something tumbled to their feet, screeching horribly.

The guard was alarmed by the noise too. Drawing his sword, he hurried toward them. "Stand back, your majesty!" he ordered.

However, Alissa recognized their visitor. "It's Bartok!" she hissed to Lia. "Balin must have returned!"

Alissa quickly spoke to the guard. "It's nothing to worry about," she reported calmly. "Only a bird. A parrot that belongs to a friend."

The guard peered at the squawking mass of feathers. "Certainly a noisy creature," he said.

"Yes, he is," agreed Alissa. "But not dangerous. We're quite all right."

The guard nodded. With a few backward glances, he returned to his post.

Once the girls were alone again, Alissa looked around for Balin. There was no sign of the wizard.

She bent closer to check on Bartok. The bird flapped his wings furiously. His feathers were dirty and mussed. And his eyes were wild—even wilder than usual.

Alissa picked up the parrot. "Settle down," she ordered. "Now tell me, where is Balin?"

Bartok glared at her. Loudly he squawked a single word: "Captured!"

"Lia!" cried Alissa in a low voice. "He has to mean Balin! Balin must have been captured!"

CHAPTER TWO

A Whispered Warning

The girls stared at the bird in disbelief. "Can you get Bartok to say anything else?" said Lia.

"Where is Balin?" Alissa asked the parrot.

Bartok merely repeated his original message: "Captured!" Then he began struggling to break free.

Alissa let go. The parrot beat his wings and took off. He flew only a few feet before landing on a low branch. From there Bartok looked back at the girls and screeched again.

"I think he wants to show us where Balin is!" exclaimed Alissa. "We have to follow!"

"I'll wait with Bartok," said Lia. "You get your father."

Alissa ran for her horse, but a shout from Lia stopped her. "Alissa, he's taking off!"

The princess whirled around to see Bartok flying across the meadow. There's no time to get my father, she thought. Bartok isn't going to stay here while I go for help.

Grabbing the reins of both horses, she called to the guard. "Please find my father! Tell him our friend in the tower is in trouble! Ask him to organize a rescue party and follow us!"

Alissa didn't wait for an answer before leaping into the saddle and wheeling her horse around. Still holding the reins of the other horse, she galloped toward Lia.

The startled guard found his tongue. "Princess! Stop!" he

shouted. "You mustn't go off alone!"

Alissa only called back to him, "Hurry! Get my father!"

The guard stared after her for a moment. Then he took off for the castle.

When Alissa reached Lia, she pulled both horses to a halt. "Get on!" she urged. "We can keep up better on horseback."

"Your father—" began Lia.

"I've sent for him," replied Alissa. "He'll follow with some of his soldiers."

Lia tied the picnic basket to her saddle. She climbed onto her horse, and the two friends thundered after Bartok.

The parrot continued to fly low, making his way over fields and meadows. Every so often, he'd perch in a tree to look around. Once he found his way, he'd take off again.

Eventually Bartok took to riding on Alissa's shoulder. If she headed in the wrong direction, he squawked in her ear.

The hunt continued for hours. The farther they rode, the more worried the girls became. At one point, Lia called to Alissa, "Do you know where we are? I've never been to this part of the kingdom before."

"Neither have I," said Alissa. "I think we'd better stop at the next inn we come to. It's getting late. And maybe my father will catch up with us tonight."

At least I hope he will, she added to herself.

～

But King Edmund didn't arrive at the small inn where Lia and Alissa spent the night. Nor did they see any sign of him during the long day that followed. For hours they traveled on—through towns, over streams, past woods.

Near sunset they stopped atop a low hill. A broad valley lay before them, bordered at the far side by a great forest.

At the edge of the forest stood a village. It appeared much like those they'd passed through earlier. Except—

"Where is everyone?" Alissa asked.

"I don't know. We haven't seen anyone on the road for a while either," observed Lia.

The girls sat in silence, watching the sky darken. Even Bartok, resting on Lia's shoulder for a change, was quiet. Gray clouds raced overhead and a chilly wind began to blow. The horses pawed at the ground restlessly.

Lia spoke softly. "This place frightens me."

"I don't like it either," said Alissa. "Still, we have to find shelter. It could be a long way to the next town."

They rode down into the village, making their way toward a small inn. But before they reached it, Bartok took to the air.

"Stop!" shouted Alissa.

The parrot ignored her cry and flew faster than ever before.

Alissa and Lia chased Bartok down the dusty road. They caught up with the bird at the opposite end of the village. He sat on a rough signpost that marked a fork in the road. One arm of the sign pointed to the west and bore the name of a town. The other arm pointed straight ahead, toward the dark forest. The lettering here was worn off and couldn't be read. That was the direction that Bartok faced.

Alissa and Lia studied the forest before them. Even here at the outskirts, the trees crowded together to shut out the light.

"We're not going in there now, Bartok," Alissa said with a shiver. "It looks like rain. And it's almost dark."

The girls turned their horses back toward the village. But

Bartok flew onward. At the edge of the forest, he roosted in a tall tree.

"Alissa, he's not coming!" called Lia.

"I really don't care," the princess sighed. Still, she brought her horse to a halt. She waited—and so did Bartok.

Finally the parrot gave an angry squawk. He flew to Lia and landed on her shoulder in a flurry of ruffled feathers.

The village remained strangely quiet as they rode back toward the inn. The small houses they passed were closed up tightly. No one came outside to peer at the travelers. In fact, the place seemed deserted.

However, the door of the inn was ajar. Alissa and Lia entered, hoping to find someone there to greet them.

The front room of the inn was cozy and welcoming. A bright fire burned in a stone fireplace. Over it hung a steaming pot. Atop the long dining table sat a dozen clean cups and bowls. Yet there wasn't a soul to be seen.

"Hello," said Alissa. There was no response.

"Hello!" she called in a louder voice. Still no response.

"No one's here," murmured Lia. "Yet everything is ready for guests."

"I think we should just stay until someone shows up," announced Alissa. "I'm hungry, and we need a place to sleep tonight."

With a tired groan, Alissa sat down to rest. Lia joined her. And Bartok flew up to find a perch high in the rafters.

Before long the silence started to make the girls nervous. Lia spoke first. "Do you think we should check the other rooms?" she asked.

Alissa's reply was interrupted by an earsplitting screech—then a loud thud.

The girls jumped to their feet. "It came from over there!" Lia said. She pointed to the other end of the room, where a door stood partly open.

At the sound of a second screech, Alissa cried, "That's Bartok!" A check of the rafters proved that she was right. The parrot was gone.

The girls rushed across the room and through the door. They found themselves in a storeroom—a very crowded storeroom. In the corner, a man was lying on the floor. Sitting on the man's chest, wings spread wide, was Bartok.

"Get him off me," begged the man.

"Come on, Bartok," Alissa ordered. The bird squawked angrily before flapping over to her shoulder.

Keeping a nervous eye on the parrot, the man got to his feet. He followed the girls out of the storeroom, grumbling about birds who attacked harmless innkeepers.

"Why didn't you answer when we called out?" asked Lia.

"Didn't hear you," the man muttered.

"I see," said Lia, clearly not believing his words. "Well, we're looking for some supper and a warm bed. So if you can—"

"We're full," the innkeeper flatly stated.

"Full!" exclaimed Alissa. "Why, there's—"

Lia interrupted by laying a hand on Alissa's arm. Gently she said, "It would be only the two of us. Surely you have room for a pair of tired travelers?"

The innkeeper's eyes slowly shifted from one girl to the other. At last he shrugged and addressed Lia. "I guess you're harmless enough, my lady. Just tell your serving girl to keep that miserable bird in hand."

Lia opened her mouth to protest. But when Alissa shook her head, Lia said nothing. The princess knew that they'd just confuse the innkeeper if they tried to explain. And it was no wonder he thought Alissa was Lia's servant. After all, she was wearing one of her older dresses, stained with picnic food. Lia, on the other hand, was neat and clean.

The innkeeper continued. "I spoke the truth, my lady. I have no rooms. All the other villagers will be here soon. If you want to stay, you must sleep on the floor."

Villagers? Alissa was puzzled. Why would the villagers, with their own homes so close, want to stay at the inn? Something strange was going on here.

"Very well, sir," said Lia.

"And the bird goes outside," the innkeeper added.

Alissa sighed. "I'll put him near the horses."

When Alissa returned, Lia was asking, "May we have something to eat, please?"

"Help yourself," the innkeeper replied, shoving two bowls at Alissa. He offered to show Lia to a seat.

Lia bent her head to hide a smile. Alissa, acting as Lia's serving maid, headed to the stewpot and filled the bowls.

While the girls ate, small groups of people entered the inn. They came in without a word, darting worried glances at one another. Even after they'd settled at the tables to eat, they had little to say.

Lia attempted to talk to a young man who sat across from her. "Good evening, sir," she greeted him.

"G-g-good day, my lady," he replied. That short response seemed enough to unsettle him. The spoon in his hand quivered and he kept his head down.

Alissa tried the old woman who sat beside her. "We thought the inn was empty when we arrived," she observed.

The woman briefly nodded. Then she pulled her shawl closer and turned away.

The remark seemed to stir someone's interest, however. A large man raised his head from his dinner. "Why are you here?" he asked angrily. "What do you want with us?"

Alissa and Lia looked at one another. What was wrong with these people?

Lia answered. "We're searching for a friend, sir. We think he may have gone into the forest at the edge of your village."

There was a gasp from someone at the far end of the table. This was followed by a whispered, "Hush!"

After that, the only sound was the scraping of spoons in bowls. No one glanced at or spoke to Alissa and Lia again.

Once dinner ended, the villagers rose and moved the table. Several people headed upstairs. Others began to bed down on the floor.

With Lia following her, Alissa went to find the innkeeper. "Is there someplace my lady could wash up?" she asked.

The innkeeper frowned and said, "There's a basin and pitcher back here." He led the two girls into a small room.

The minute the door closed behind him, Alissa spoke. "What do you suppose is going on?" she asked. "Why is everyone so unfriendly?"

"They seem frightened," said Lia. "Especially when I mentioned the forest. Maybe we shouldn't go into the woods, Alissa. At least not until your father arrives."

"We can't wait. We have to help Balin. I'm not sure what's happened to him. But I know it's nothing good. If Bartok goes into that forest, I'm following him."

Lia knew there was no point in trying to convince her friend to do otherwise. Lia loved the old wizard too. But the tie between Balin and Alissa was even more special. Balin had chosen Alissa to be his student. And the princess knew his lessons were a great gift. She would do anything to save him from harm—just as he would do for her.

So Lia nodded. "Then I'm going with you."

The girls went back to the main room to find a spot to sleep.

But sleep didn't come easily to the princess. She lay awake long after the fire was only glowing ashes. She found it hard to get comfortable on the inn's stone floor.

As she rolled over for at least the tenth time, a whispered conversation caught Alissa's attention. She held her breath and listened.

"Should we warn them?" asked a voice.

"About what?" said a second. Alissa felt sure it was the innkeeper speaking now.

"You know what! About the storms—and those who've disappeared. Those girls should know of the dangers!"

The reply was cold. "I say we keep our mouths shut. If they're foolish enough to go into the forest, let them. It won't be our problem. They'll never be seen again."

CHAPTER THREE

The Forest of Fear

aint rays of light told Alissa that morning had arrived. It had been a long, restless night. The innkeeper's words—even more than the hard floor—had kept her awake.

She groaned and sat up. It appeared that everyone else was still asleep. Not that it matters, she thought. We'll get no help from these people.

Alissa poked Lia, who slept beside her. When her friend's eyes opened, Alissa held a finger to her lips. She picked up their basket and got to her feet.

With one look at Alissa's worried face, Lia rose quietly. She followed her friend, stepping carefully around sleeping figures. Alissa dropped a gold coin on the table before slipping out the door.

Lia remained silent until they reached Bartok and their horses. There she grabbed Alissa's sleeve. "What's going on?" she whispered. "Why are we sneaking out?"

"Because there's something very wrong here," explained Alissa. She went on to report what she'd overheard.

"'Never be seen again!'" repeated Lia, swallowing a gasp. "Do you think it's true?"

"I don't know," admitted Alissa. "But the innkeeper certainly sounded convinced. Besides, in a terrible kind of way, it makes sense."

"What do you mean?"

"Come on," was Alissa's answer. "We can talk once we're away from here a bit."

The princess untied her horse and lifted Bartok onto her saddle. The parrot rode calmly until they reached the edge of town. Then he took to his wings and came to rest once again on the signpost. He gazed into the forest and croaked, "Captured!"

"All right, Alissa," said Lia. "Now tell me what you meant. What makes sense?"

Alissa motioned toward the parrot and the dark woods behind him. "The forest. How frightened everyone is. Balin being missing. And what Bartok keeps saying. I'm sure that Balin is a prisoner in this forest."

"I agree. Though who could have captured him?" asked Lia. "Balin's magic is so strong."

"Well, he has at least one very powerful enemy. Somebody who's evil enough to frighten a whole village. And who nearly overpowered Balin once before."

Lia went pale. "You mean the sorcerer?" she breathed. "The one who tried to ruin the peace treaty in Arcadia?"

Alissa nodded. "I'm afraid so."

"But you kept that from happening," said Lia. "With Balin's help."

"Yes," said Alissa. "However, Balin warned me that we weren't rid of the sorcerer forever."

"What else did Balin tell you about him?"

"Not much," Alissa replied. "He did say the sorcerer often went by the name of Mordock. And that he could take any form he wanted. That's why we had no idea who he was when we fought him in Arcadia. Not until it was almost too late to stop him."

"Mordock," Lia whispered. Her eyes traveled from the twisted trees to the dark, swirling clouds overhead.

Alissa noticed her friend shiver. She again thought about what might lie ahead. Slowly she came to a decision.

"Lia, I think you should wait here in the village," she said. "To show my father where I've gone."

Lia gave Alissa a shocked glance. "And let you go alone? I can't do that!"

"If Mordock is in the forest, we have no idea what we'll find," said Alissa. "But we do know it's going to be dangerous. We knew that even before I overheard the innkeeper."

"All the more reason why you shouldn't go alone!" declared Lia. "Though I'm not sure what chance we have against Mordock."

"I'm not sure either," admitted Alissa. "I do know that Balin is in danger. So I have to find him as soon as possible."

The girls' argument was interrupted by a cry from Bartok. They turned to see him taking to the air.

"Lia! He's headed straight into the forest!" Alissa cried. "I can't lose sight of him."

The princess took off. And without a moment's hesitation, Lia followed her.

The girls hadn't gone far into the woods before the road became a rough, overgrown path. Once, Alissa glanced back the way they'd come. No trace of the village could be seen. In fact, the path they'd taken seemed to have vanished.

17

The way grew so narrow that the girls had to dismount and lead their horses. Bartok stayed ahead, flying low to the ground. From time to time, he perched on a branch to wait. Whenever they'd catch up, he'd start down the trail again.

The twisted pines gradually gave way to huge trees, many of them thorn-covered. Meanwhile, the storm clouds grew thicker and darker. So little light reached the forest floor that the girls could barely see the path. The air hung still and heavy around them.

Suddenly a mighty gust of wind slammed into the tree-tops. Thunder growled and lightning crackled overhead.

"No wonder the villagers are frightened!" gasped Lia. "This forest must be enchanted!"

Alissa caught her breath as the wind pounded the trees. Lightning cut through the branches like swords. Then, without warning, great hailstones dropped from the sky.

"We've got to find some cover!" yelled Alissa.

Lia peered ahead. "Over this way, Alissa!" she called.

Leading their horses, the girls dashed toward the shelter of an overhanging rock.

But before they reached safety, lightning struck a towering oak in front of them. The tree groaned, and sparks shot from its upper branches. Whinnying in terror, the horses pulled free and galloped off.

Alissa was about to give chase when an earsplitting screech brought her up short. In horror she watched as the huge tree split in half—and started falling toward them.

CHAPTER FOUR

Captives of the Castle

ia!" Alissa screamed.

The princess grabbed her friend, pulling her to the ground and away from the tree. Together they rolled beneath the shelf of rock.

They barely made it before the tree hit the earth. Its crash echoed through the woods.

As the noise died away, Alissa lowered her arms. Inches from her face was a snarl of branches.

Alissa pushed the branches aside and struggled to her feet. Lia slowly did the same.

"Are you all right?" Alissa asked.

"I think so," answered Lia. "Thanks to you." She brushed leaves and twigs from her dress. "How about you?"

"A few scrapes," announced Alissa, pushing her way past the fallen tree.

"Well, Bartok is here," said the princess. "But our horses are gone."

"They're probably halfway back to Arcadia by now," remarked Lia.

"Maybe that's good," said Alissa.

Lia shot her a startled look. "Why?"

"If my father sees our horses, he'll know we're in trouble."

Lia nodded. "And with any luck, he'll be able to follow

20

their trail into the forest." She glanced up at the sky. "I guess it's safe to go on. I think the worst of the storm is over."

"Let's hurry," said Alissa. "I have a feeling Balin's not too far from here."

At the mention of the wizard's name, Bartok stirred. "Captured!" he repeated. Then he flew off once more.

For the next several hours, the girls trailed the parrot. On foot they found it harder to keep up with him. However, Bartok always waited when they fell too far behind.

Finally the parrot landed on a branch. He fixed his beak straight ahead and sat without moving.

The girls inched closer. "There must be something up ahead," whispered Alissa.

They crept along until they reached Bartok. "Look!" cried Lia in a low voice.

Ahead of them, the forest opened up into a clearing. In the middle of that clearing rose a castle of deep black stone.

There was no doubt in Alissa's mind that this was Mordock's castle. Everything about it was gloomy, dark, and frightening. A wide, muddy moat circled the castle. Thorns and brambles clawed at the towering walls. And at the gate marched dozens of guards, all oddly silent. The only thing to be heard was the dull clank of their weapons against armor.

The girls retreated to the shelter of the thick forest. Once they were hidden, Lia asked, "What should we do now?"

"Balin must be inside that castle," Alissa declared. "At least that's what Bartok seems to be trying to tell us. Which means we have to get inside too."

"But there are guards everywhere," Lia pointed out. "Though they won't be the worst of our problems if Mordock is behind this."

"I know," replied the princess. "'Let's just watch for a while. I want to see what the guards do."

The girls edged back toward the clearing. Hiding in the bushes, they studied the castle and its guards. They watched until darkness began to fall over the clearing. Yet they saw nothing that might help them rescue Balin.

Alissa shivered in the cool evening air. Tapping Lia on the shoulder, she motioned toward the forest behind them. Lia nodded and followed her away from the clearing.

Once they were at a distance, Alissa stopped. "I guess we'll have to spend the night out here," she said. "But where? It's getting cold. And we don't have a thing to eat. The picnic leftovers disappeared along with our horses."

"I spotted a hollow under a fallen tree not far from here," said Lia. "We could sleep there. At least we'll stay dry if it starts to rain again." She glanced up at the gray clouds.

"We don't have a choice," admitted Alissa. "So let's go."

Lia headed farther back into the forest, with Alissa and Bartok behind her.

By nightfall, Alissa and Lia had settled beneath the tree. Cold, tired, and hungry, they found little comfort in the inky darkness. Still, they were too tired to stay awake for long.

Alissa didn't stir until morning crept slowly into the forest. It wasn't the dim sunlight that awakened her, however. Something else had startled her out of a sound sleep.

For several moments, Alissa lay motionless, listening. Then she heard it again—a rustling noise. It sounded like it was nearby.

"Alissa, are you awake? Did you hear that?" whispered Lia. She raised herself up on one elbow.

"I heard something," said Alissa quietly.

22

Bartok stirred restlessly, and Alissa wrapped her hand around his beak.

The noise grew louder. Leaves crunched. Twigs snapped. Whoever was out there was moving faster now.

The next thing the girls knew, someone charged into their hiding place—and into Alissa. Bartok flew out of her hands, giving a low squawk of fear.

Alissa silenced a gasp. It was only a boy. A boy who was probably no older than she and Lia.

As he untangled himself from Alissa, the boy whispered, "Don't give me away."

Alissa whispered back, "Give you away? What are you talking—"

At the sound of marching feet, Alissa fell silent. Through the branches of the fallen tree, she caught the gleam of armor. Several soldiers were coming toward them from the direction of the castle.

The guards neared the tree. But they went right past, deeper into the forest.

When the guards were gone, Alissa's attention returned to the boy. "Who are you? What are you doing here?"

"I'm Crispin," he answered. "And I'm hiding, of course. Aren't you?"

"Well, yes, we are," admitted Alissa. "Do you realize you might have led those soldiers right to us?"

"But I didn't, did I?" replied the boy. He straightened his shoulders with pride and grinned. "I'm much too smart for the likes of them.

That's why I was able to escape from the castle."

Alissa had been studying Crispin as he talked. Now that the guards were gone, the boy's eyes shone with excitement. Still, he hardly looked the brave hero he seemed to think he was. His tunic was torn and filthy. His shaggy blond hair was uncombed. And what appeared to be vegetable peelings peeked out from under his collar and sleeves.

Hero or not, the boy's words interested Alissa. "You escaped from the castle?" she repeated.

"I certainly did," said Crispin. "Not even Lord Mordock's sorcery could stop me."

"Mordock!" cried Lia.

"It *is* Mordock's castle!" exclaimed Alissa. "I knew it!"

Crispin drew back, his grin fading. "You know about him?" he said uneasily. "How can that be? Mordock keeps his identity a secret to everyone outside the walls of Grimrock."

He got to his feet and began to inch away. "You must be sorcerers too. That would explain the bird," he said.

"Oh, sit down," said Alissa. "We're not sorcerers. And the bird is nothing to fear."

Bartok flapped his wings and ordered, "Begone!"

"Friendly creature, isn't he?" Crispin muttered. But he sat once again.

"Tell me who you are then," he demanded. "And what you're doing here."

Alissa told him their names. She didn't mention that she was a princess, however. She doubted Crispin would believe her. "As for why we're here, we're trying to find a friend of ours," she said.

"We think Mordock is keeping him prisoner," added Lia.

"There's a good chance of that," said Crispin. "Grimrock

is filled with prisoners. A lot of people from my own village were captured. The guards took me many weeks ago when I was gathering wood in the forest."

"Are there other prisoners besides the people from your village?" asked Alissa.

"Some," Crispin responded. "What's your friend's name?"

"Balin," said Alissa. "He's very old, with a long white beard. Have you seen him?" She held her breath, waiting for Crispin's answer.

The boy thought for a bit. "No, I don't think I have. If he's old, he may be in the dungeons. Mordock has little use for prisoners who can't do a hard day's work. He wants them young and strong. Like me," he said with another grin.

"There's one thing I don't understand," commented Lia. "Why is the sorcerer taking so many prisoners?"

"Mordock hasn't shared his plans with me," replied Crispin. "So I can't answer that question. I *can* tell you that things have gotten worse since I was first captured."

"What do you mean?" asked Alissa.

Crispin settled himself more comfortably in the hiding spot. "Well, for a while, I worked in the stables." He paused and smiled. "Until one of the guards realized I was digging an escape route under the stalls. After that I ended up working in the kitchen. They could keep a closer eye on me there."

Alissa and Lia traded glances. Crispin certainly hadn't let Mordock's powers frighten him. Not like the people they'd met in the village.

Crispin continued. "But things were changing even before I was sent to work in the kitchen. I remember that Mordock went away for several days. It was right after he returned that the terrible storms started. And that's when the guards began bringing in more prisoners. It's also when I first saw the monsters in the moat."

Alissa shivered. All these changes must have taken place after Mordock had captured Balin. Clearly the sorcerer's evil powers had grown.

She stared off in the direction of the castle. "I guess we have no choice," she said. "We'll have to get inside and free Balin."

"Get inside!" echoed Crispin. "You can't get inside! Not unless you're captured!"

"You got out," said Alissa. "Maybe we can sneak in the same way."

"I don't think so," laughed Crispin. "I slid down the waste chute in the kitchen. There's no way you can slide up!"

"That explains the peelings," remarked Lia. Crispin grinned and removed a piece of carrot from his tunic.

"All right," Alissa said. "If that way won't work, I'll find another. Tell me about the castle."

She began to shower Crispin with questions. How many guards were there? What was the castle like on the inside? How were the captives being treated?

Crispin answered as best he could. "I can't be certain how many guards there are. In their armor, they all look alike. They never say a word. In fact, they don't seem human."

He went on to explain that he hadn't seen much of the inside of Grimrock. "Remember, I didn't work in the kitchen for long. And I certainly didn't learn much from the servants there. We weren't supposed to speak to each other. Not that that stopped me, of course," he said boldly. "But there are many who are too scared to open their mouths."

Crispin added, "Even when Mordock isn't about, Gerda is

26

there to see that everyone obeys orders without question. She's the housekeeper who runs the castle for Mordock. She's as bad as he is."

Alissa caught Lia's eye. She knew her friend was thinking the same thing she was. This was how Mordock treated the villagers he'd captured. How much worse he must be treating Balin, his old enemy.

Suddenly Bartok opened and closed his beak with a sharp warning click. Crispin stopped talking at once. The soldiers were returning.

After they go by, thought Alissa, Crispin can get out of here. I'll give him a message in case he meets up with my father. Then tonight, when it's dark, Lia and I will try to find a way into the castle.

The tramping of feet slowed, then stopped. Alissa, Lia, and Crispin all froze.

Suddenly a wash of light flowed into their hiding place. Alissa fearfully looked upward. Two guards had lifted the huge tree trunk away from the rock where it rested.

With a combination of terror and curiosity, the princess stared at Mordock's men. The soldiers' shiny armor hid their features—except for their eyes. These were dark, cold, and empty.

In frightening silence, guards moved forward to seize the three captives.

CHAPTER FIVE

Mordock's Welcome

Bartok took to the air with a loud cry. However, the guards paid no attention to the parrot. Without a word, they forced Alissa, Lia, and Crispin to their feet.

Crispin struggled, but he was soon overpowered. The firm arm on her own shoulder warned Alissa that there was no chance of escape.

The three captives were herded toward the castle. At the edge of the moat, the guards paused. Bubbles rose up through the muddy water and softly popped. A sharp snout broke the surface for an instant, jaws snapping and teeth flashing. The monster quickly disappeared with the flick of its huge tail.

Alissa's heart sank. Were they going to be thrown into the dark water of the moat?

Then the great drawbridge began to creak downward. When it fell into place, a soldier pushed Alissa across.

Once they were inside, the drawbridge was raised. Alissa watched the forest outside disappear inch by inch. Finally the bridge shut with a thump.

The princess studied the hallway where they stood. Torches—few and far between—dimly lit the scene. The walls and floors were damp and cold. There were no rugs or tapestries to brighten the stone.

They started down the hall. At the first corner, one guard gripped Crispin's arm. He roughly dragged the boy down a flight of stairs that led into darkness.

Next it was Alissa and Lia's turn. A few more steps brought them to a heavy door set into the wall. A guard unlocked this room and motioned them inside. They heard a key rattle in the lock. Then the sound of footsteps gradually faded away.

"Now what do we do?" asked Lia.

"I don't know," admitted Alissa as she began to explore their prison. It was a small room, made entirely of stone. The blocks of the wall fitted together so closely that hardly a crack could be seen. The only light came from a barred opening near the top of the door.

Alissa sank to the floor, her back against the cold stone. Lia joined her.

At last Alissa broke the silence. "I'm sorry to have dragged you into this, Lia. We should have waited in the village for my father. We won't be of any help to Balin caged up in this cell."

"Well, at least we've managed to find a way to get into Grimrock," Lia said. "Though I'm afraid we may be left here to starve."

"That won't happen," said Alissa. "From what Crispin said, I'm sure Mordock will put us to work."

"Something to look forward to," said Lia. She managed a smile, which Alissa returned. It was clear that Lia was frightened but trying not to show it. Just like Alissa.

An hour or more passed before they heard footsteps again. Someone was walking toward the cell door.

As the girls rose to their feet, Alissa reached for Lia's hand. Holding her breath, the princess watched the door open.

A guard stood there, blocking the light from the hallway. Behind him waited a shadowy figure.

"Well, well, what have we here?" asked a silky voice.

A man stepped past the guard. He was tall, with broad shoulders and powerful arms. Built like a soldier, thought Alissa. Yet his face was harder than any solider's she'd ever seen. He stared at them with cold black eyes, his lips curled in distaste. There wasn't a drop of warmth about him—not even in his clothes. From head to toe, he was draped in black.

This has to be Mordock, thought Alissa as the man moved closer. Though he certainly looks nothing like he did when I saw him before.

Suddenly fear rocked her. He's seen us before as well, she thought. What if he recognizes us? He'll know we're here to rescue Balin.

She lowered her head, letting her hair fall forward over her face.

"More foolish peasants," Mordock observed. "When will you learn not to wander into my forest?"

Alissa slowly let out her breath. She realized that with her muddy face and dress, she'd never be taken for a princess. And dirt had dulled Lia's flaming hair. In spite of his powers, Mordock saw what he expected to see.

The sorcerer bowed and his smile widened. "Welcome to Grimrock, ladies," he said. "It will be an honor to have you work here. I'm sure you'll enjoy my castle."

In a flash, the smile faded and his voice hardened. "Now

it's time to earn your keep. If you want to eat, that is."

With that, he left the room. At once the guard stepped forward, pointing his spear toward the door. He herded the girls into the hall and down the stairs. The same stairs that Crispin had taken.

A tall woman, her black hair streaked with gray, waited at the bottom. With her arms folded across her chest, she stared at them with dark, unfriendly eyes. "Come!" she ordered sharply. She waved the guard off and led the way down the hall.

Silently, the girls followed the woman. Soon she stopped and pushed them ahead of her into a large, well-furnished room. Then she entered and planted herself in a cushioned chair.

"I am Gerda," she announced. "Second only to Lord Mordock in this castle. Whatever I tell you, you will do. Without question. Without hesitation."

She glared at the girls and motioned them forward. "Come here where I can see you clearly."

The housekeeper studied Lia, then Alissa. "You seem no better than the rest of these miserable villagers," she sniffed.

"Understand this," Gerda continued. "You'll find that there are few locked doors inside the castle walls. That's because they aren't needed. Once the drawbridge is raised, there is no escape from Grimrock. Don't waste time even thinking about it."

Forgetting her fear, Alissa asked, "What about Crispin?"

"Silence!" roared Gerda, her face clouding with anger. "You may be sure that his escape route no longer exists."

She went on in a quieter voice. "Your work is to be done to my satisfaction. If it is, you'll receive two meals a day. Both are to be taken in your chambers. And if your work does not please me—or Lord Mordock—you'll pay dearly!"

She waited for her words to sink in before continuing. "Not very long ago, Grimrock was in ruins. The castle was almost eaten up by the forest itself. But Lord Mordock brought it back to life. Because of him, Grimrock is once again a great castle. A fortress of magic, ruled by a master whose powers are without equal."

Gerda bent closer to the two girls. "Remember one thing: Mordock put me in charge. I intend to see that everything is done as he wishes. Everything," she repeated.

The housekeeper smiled unpleasantly. "Now let's see how valuable you will be to me—and to his lordship."

She asked question after question. What is the best way to scrub a stone floor? How do you prepare wool for spinning? What makes the finest wicks for candles? And so on.

Lia was able to give answers that Gerda would accept. But Alissa's replies displeased her. The only question the princess could answer was one about how to scrub pots. That she had done before, for Balin.

"You know almost nothing," said Gerda to Alissa. "What have you been doing, girl? Reading books and learning fine manners? Not a chance from the looks of you, I'd say. Perhaps you're simpleminded. Well, no matter. Any fool can learn to be a kitchen maid. Even you."

Gerda stood up. "Follow me..." She paused and snapped her fingers. "Your names. What are your names? I hope you can answer that question," she said, eyeing Alissa.

For a moment, Alissa thought of using a false name. However, she decided that Mordock would probably never hear her name anyway. Even if he did, he wouldn't connect her with the princess of Arcadia.

She took a deep breath and said, "My name is Alissa."

"And I am Lia."

Gerda's only response was to snarl, "Come with me."

The housekeeper marched to the other end of her sitting room. There she threw open a door to reveal the largest kitchen Alissa had ever seen.

The place was crowded with workers—men and women, boys and girls. All looked dirty and tired. And all worked in silence, with eyes cast down. No one paid the least attention to the two new captives. A sense of hopelessness filled the huge room.

Gerda paused before a great stone fireplace. The fire was cold, and dozens of iron pots sat atop the ashes.

Giving Alissa an icy glare, Gerda said, "You can scrub these pots. Apparently that's all you're suited for."

To Lia she said, "You'll be working upstairs. We'll soon see if your spinning skills are as fine as you say." With that, Gerda headed across the kitchen.

Lia glanced at the housekeeper's stiff back. She leaned close to Alissa. "I'll find you somehow," she promised.

"Lia!" barked Gerda.

Alissa sadly watched as Lia rushed after the housekeeper. She'd never felt quite so alone before. With a faint sigh, she rolled up her sleeves and began scrubbing.

Even with Gerda out of the room, no one spoke to Alissa or looked her way. She scrubbed for hours, until her hands were rough and sore. Several times during the afternoon,

Gerda came by to check Alissa's work. Each time the house-keeper complained that some pots weren't clean enough. Then she'd order the princess to redo them.

At the day's end, Gerda appeared once more. When she clapped her hands, everyone stopped working. They gathered in the middle of the kitchen, lining up in front of the house-keeper. Alissa took a place at the end of the line.

One by one, the captives filed past Gerda. Each received some bread and a cup of water. Most already carried their own tin mugs.

Finally Alissa's turn came. Gerda handed her a cup of water and a hunk of bread. The water was lukewarm, and the bread was stale. Even so, Alissa was thankful that she had anything at all to eat and drink.

She followed the others out of the kitchen. In the hallway, several guards waited. They led the captives down several passages until they reached a row of cells. By ones and twos, the captives split up and entered the rooms.

Alissa hesitated until a guard motioned to her. He opened a door and shoved her toward it.

Clutching her bread and water, Alissa crept into her prison cell.

CHAPTER SIX

A Brush with Danger

lissa blinked in the darkness. The only light came from the torches in the hallway outside.

As her eyes became used to the dim light, Alissa noticed a shape in the corner. Someone was already in the cell!

"Alissa?" asked a soft voice.

"Oh, Lia! Thank goodness!" cried the princess. She rushed toward her friend. The two girls hugged, overjoyed to find themselves together.

"Did you get some food?" asked Alissa.

"Nothing but this," replied Lia. She too had a cup of water and a hunk of bread.

"It's not much, is it?" sighed Alissa. "Especially if we're expected to work so hard."

The girls sat on the thin mat that covered most of the floor. Both were hungry, so they began eating at once. Between bites, they shared their experiences.

"I didn't actually do much spinning," said Lia. "I mostly ran back and forth, fetching things."

"Well, I certainly did plenty of scrubbing," sighed Alissa. "Sometimes I cleaned the same pot over and over. I couldn't seem to satisfy Gerda."

"She kept checking on me too," said Lia.

"Whenever she was gone, I tried to scout around the kitchen," said Alissa. "To see if there was a way out. But I couldn't spot anything. Gerda told the truth about the waste chute. It's been boarded up."

Her words reminded them of Crispin and how he'd been dragged away.

"I wonder what happened to poor Crispin?" said Lia with a shiver.

"Whatever it was, I'm sure it wasn't good," said Alissa.

The princess got to her feet. With a shake of her head, she studied their chamber. "I guess this dirty mat is where we sleep," she observed. "I wish we had water for washing up."

"And a brush for our hair," added Lia.

Alissa touched her messy curls. As she ran her fingers through her hair, they caught on something. It was her locket—the one Balin had given her.

Thoughtfully she pulled it out from under her dress. "Do you think I should hide my locket under the mat?" she asked Lia. "To make sure that Gerda and Mordock don't see it?"

"I don't know. Didn't Balin tell you to wear it all the time?"

"Yes," admitted Alissa. "He said not to take it off until he told me to."

"I think that answers your question," said Lia. "Let me make sure it doesn't show."

She helped Alissa tuck the necklace in. "It's a good thing your hair hides the chain," she noted.

Once the locket was back in place, Alissa walked over to the chamber door. Standing on tiptoe, she peered through the bars. Then she leaned against the door to peer down the hall.

"Lia!" she cried in a low voice. "The door moved. It isn't locked!"

"It doesn't need to be," said Lia bitterly. "Gerda warned us there was no escape."

"Maybe we can't get out of the castle," remarked Alissa. "But we can explore inside a bit. We might be able to find Balin. I wonder..."

She opened the heavy door slightly. Then, ever so slowly, she peeked outside.

Far down the hall stood a guard, facing away from her. When he began to turn, Alissa ducked back into her cell.

"There's a guard out there," she reported, closing the door quietly behind her.

"That means we definitely won't be doing any exploring," said Lia.

"He might not be there every night," Alissa murmured. Her voice trailed off in a mighty yawn. "Well, I'm too worn out right now to think about it."

"We'd better get some sleep," agreed Lia. "We're in for more hard work tomorrow."

The girls curled up next to each other. Lia was asleep in moments. But Alissa lay awake for a while. She wished with all her might that her father would find her—and soon.

She heard the guard walk past once. Twice. By the third time he made his rounds, she too had fallen into a heavy sleep.

~

It was as dark as night when the girls were awakened. For a moment, Alissa couldn't remember where she was.

The clanging of a stick against metal reminded her. It was

Gerda, banging on the barred door of each cell. As she did so, she cried, "Up with you! There's work to be done!"

Alissa moaned. She and Lia had barely struggled to their feet before Gerda flung open their door. Behind her stood a guard carrying a basket and a jug.

"Hurry up," the housekeeper ordered. The girls quickly moved forward to collect their bread and water. Then Gerda was off to the next cell.

They barely had time to finish their poor breakfast before the guard was back. He motioned them into the hall, where they joined the other captives. Lia was herded upstairs with one group. Alissa headed back to the kitchen with the rest.

It proved to be another long workday. When Alissa and Lia met in their chamber that night, they traded stories.

Alissa had again spent the entire time scrubbing dirty pots. But Lia had been moved from the spinning room to the candlemaker's shop.

Then Alissa reported her good news. "I saw Crispin!" she announced. "He was working on the other side of the kitchen. While Gerda was out of the room, he grinned at me."

"Thank goodness he's all right," said Lia.

After eating, Alissa stationed herself by the door. For a long time she stood there, staring out the bars. Lia started to say something once, but Alissa laid a finger to her lips.

Finally she turned to her friend. "I've figured it out!" she said. "I've been counting how long it takes the guard to make his rounds."

"And?" said Lia.

"I think we can get down the hall before he spots us."

"Are you sure?" asked Lia.

"No," admitted Alissa. "But we have to do something, Lia.

40

We can't simply wait here, hoping my father and his soldiers will show up."

"All right. Let's try it," said Lia.

After the guard passed by once more, they tiptoed into the hall. Quickly they headed in the opposite direction. As the girls hurried down the passage, they counted ten doors along the wall. Around the corner, they found still other rooms.

Alissa, who'd been keeping track of time, motioned to her friend. The guard was due back any minute. As they turned around, they heard his footsteps.

The girls froze. What should they do now?

Suddenly the door beside them swung open. A hand reached out and dragged Lia inside. Alissa followed.

Before the guard rounded the corner, they were safely inside the cell. The girls crouched in the darkness, listening to the guard walk past.

Then a familiar voice said, "I see you're still anxious to explore Grimrock."

"Crispin?" cried Alissa. "Is it really you?"

The boy moved closer to the door. There the weak light from the hallway lit his features. "It's me all right," he replied. "Back in my usual cell after a night in the dungeons."

"The dungeons!" Lia breathed. "What are they like?"

Crispin shuddered. "It's a strange place. As dark as the bottom of a well, for one thing. Lots of rusty locked doors. Cold and wet too. But that's nothing. There are strange noises and slimy things in the corners—"

He cut himself short and gave a shaky laugh. "Still, it'll take more than a few sorcerer's tricks to cure me of trying to escape."

"Did you see our friend?" Alissa asked.

Crispin shook his head. "No. Though I did ask another

prisoner about him. He mentioned that there was a captive who especially interested Mordock."

"Alissa," breathed Lia. "Do you think...?"

"Yes, it might be Balin," replied Alissa. She asked Crispin to describe the dungeons and how to reach them.

Lia broke in. "Alissa, we have to get back to our cell. Before the guard hears us in here."

Alissa nodded. "We're down the other passage. If it's all right with you, we'll come back later."

Crispin nodded. "I'll be here. At least until I figure out another way to escape. And I will escape, I promise you."

The girls opened the door a crack. Seeing no sign of the guard, they darted to their own chamber. There they sank to the floor in relief.

"Thanks to Crispin, we now know that Balin is probably in the dungeons," Alissa said.

Lia nodded. "So how do we get down there? And out again? Remember what Crispin said. The dungeon is one place in the castle where there are lots of locked doors."

"I don't have a plan yet," Alissa admitted. "But if we can come up with one, I'm sure Crispin will help us. Then maybe we can help him too."

～

Next morning Alissa discovered she had a new chore. She was to scrub the floor in the castle's banquet hall.

Before leaving Alissa to her task, Gerda delivered a stern warning. "Get this job done at once. And be sure it's done right the first time. I want you out of the way before Lord Mordock comes by."

Head down, Alissa nodded meekly. She had no wish to see

Mordock either.

The princess began scrubbing. Not until she'd finished half the floor did she dare to peek about. When she was sure she was alone, Alissa got up off her hands and knees. "Time for a little exploring," she whispered to herself.

Ahead of her, a set of double doors rose toward the ceiling. From what Gerda had said, Alissa knew that this was the entrance to Mordock's study.

If only I could sneak in there, she thought. I'm sure I'd find something helpful. A book of spells, perhaps. Or some magical ingredients.

Alissa leaned over. Placing one eye against the keyhole, she tried to see into the room.

At the sound of footsteps behind her, Alissa jerked her head away. She scrambled back, dropping to her knees and grabbing for her brush.

But the brush was slippery with soap. Alissa's hand slid off, sending the scrub brush skidding out of control. It shot across the floor in the direction of the footsteps.

Alissa made a mad dive for the brush. She caught it—just as it came to rest against a black-booted foot.

Alissa slowly looked up. The boot belonged to Mordock!

CHAPTER SEVEN

Deep in the Dungeons

ordock stared down at Alissa, his black eyes cold and unreadable. Behind him stood Gerda. The housekeeper had her hands on her hips and a steely frown on her face.

Alissa didn't move. In fact, she hardly took a breath.

"I must say," Mordock began, "I've never seen one so clumsy. Is this how you train my servants, Gerda?"

Fury flashed in the housekeeper's eyes. Still, when she spoke to the sorcerer, her voice was calm and respectful. "I'll see that the girl is properly punished, your lordship." She gave the sorcerer a nervous smile.

The smile Mordock gave her in return held no warmth. But when his icy glance moved to Alissa, his eyes suddenly filled with pleasure.

He likes the fact that I'm frightened, Alissa realized. That made her angry—and her anger made her brave.

He doesn't recognize me, she thought. Not with my dirty face and dress. So I'm not going to let him treat me like this.

Brush in hand, Alissa rose to her feet. She curtsied and spoke directly to the sorcerer. "My apologies, sir," she said. "I'm sure you'll forgive one who is unused to serving such a great lord."

For a moment, Mordock simply stood there. Then he

threw his head back and laughed.

As quickly as it had started, Mordock's laughter died. "So, Gerda," he said. "Who is this bold maid?"

"Her name is Alissa, my lord," replied Gerda.

"Alissa," repeated the sorcerer. "Well, I see you've yet to strike fear into her heart."

"I'll soon take care of that," the housekeeper declared.

Gerda moved toward Alissa. But Mordock signaled her to stop. "Wait," he ordered. His eyes slowly swept over Alissa.

"Not quite the silly scrub maid you seem," he said at long last. "Interesting."

Then, with a swirl of his robes, Mordock pushed past Alissa and entered his study.

Once the door closed behind him, Gerda's respectful look turned to rage. "Make a fool of me, will you?" she snarled, grabbing Alissa's arm. Without another word, she rushed her captive back toward the kitchen.

Alissa didn't have long to wonder what her punishment would be. As soon as they reached the kitchen, Gerda spat out orders.

"All right—you with the quick tongue—pay attention," she snapped. "It's clear that you need more practice scrubbing floors. And you shall get it. In the dungeons."

Alissa couldn't help feeling a little frightened. Crispin's words about the strange sights and sounds of the dungeons came back to her. As brave as he'd sounded, it was plain that he'd found them a fearsome place.

Gerda noticed the expression on Alissa's face and laughed. "I warned you to remain silent. Perhaps this will teach you to obey me."

She called to a guard. "Take her down to the dungeons,"

she ordered. "And leave her there. She's to scrub every inch of the floor."

The guard led Alissa out of the kitchen. Through halls, under archways, and around corners he guided her. Then they went down a twisting stairway, moving even deeper beneath the castle.

At the bottom of the stairs stood a great door of solid iron, bolted shut by a sturdy lock.

Watching the guard reach for the key at his waist, Alissa shivered. Crispin was right. The air down here was cold and clammy. A heavy silence hung over everything.

With a click, the lock fell open. The guard shoved Alissa forward and slammed the door behind her. The sound echoed off the stone walls.

For a minute, Alissa stood still, uneasily studying the dark hallway. The passage in front of her was lighted by only two torches. Weird echoes and ghostly mists drifted out of the darkness.

Alissa straightened her shoulders. Well, I wanted to get into the dungeons, she thought. And I did.

With shaking hands, she put down her bucket. I'd better at least pretend to work, she decided. Just in case Gerda comes to check.

Alissa poured water on the filthy floor and got down on her knees. While she scrubbed, her eyes darted from side to side. She noted that the dungeon appeared to be L-shaped. The passage where Alissa worked ran between two rows of locked cells. The walls facing out were made of iron bars that ran from floor to ceiling. However, it was too dark to see deep inside the cells. About a hundred feet away, the hall bent sharply to the right.

Feeling bolder now, Alissa got to her feet. She gave her bucket a loud rattle. She hoped that the noise would attract the attention of the prisoners. Perhaps one of them would know something about Balin. Perhaps one of them would *be* Balin.

Shuffling footsteps told the princess that at least one cell was occupied. A pair of sad eyes peered out at her.

"Hello," Alissa whispered. "Can you help me?"

The eyes blinked and widened. Then the prisoner backed away.

"Won't you please talk to me?" begged Alissa. There was no response.

Bucket still in hand, Alissa moved down the passage. But she had no more luck at other cells. Several prisoners came forward to stare at her with hollow, fearful eyes. Yet none would talk to her.

Alissa reached the bend in the hall and edged around the corner. I'll bet this is where Mordock has Balin locked up, she thought.

An angry hiss stopped the princess in her tracks. Lying directly in her path was a gigantic snake. Its body was as thick around as Alissa's waist.

Tongue flickering, the creature raised its huge head. It began to slither toward her.

At first Alissa was frozen with fear. The snake was almost upon her before she moved. Without thinking, she used the only weapon she had. She hurled the bucket of dirty water at the snake.

At once the snake exploded in a burst of sparks. The sparks rose into the air, then fell to the cold stone floor. There they sputtered and sizzled for several moments. Finally the

flashes died away, leaving nothing but a black scar on the floor near the bucket.

Trembling, Alissa stared at what remained of the snake. "Mordock," she murmured. "It must have been one of his magical creatures."

Alissa crept around the corner once again. She stepped carefully, expecting more surprises. But other than a few rats, she saw no sign of life.

This passage was lined with cells too. The cell at the end of the corridor immediately caught Alissa's attention. Unlike the others, this one was closed off with a heavy wooden door. The only opening was a small barred peephole.

Heart thumping, Alissa hurried to the end of the hall. She peeked through the opening—and discovered that the first door led to two more. These were built in the barred style of the other cells.

Beyond the third door, she spotted someone lying on the floor, facing the wall. Alissa could see that the prisoner wore a familiar robe of bright scarlet.

"Balin!" she cried softly. There was no answer.

Alissa yanked at the heavy door, but it didn't budge. "Balin," she called again.

Though the figure didn't move, there was a response this time. A rusty voice spoke from behind Alissa.

"Just who might you be?"

Alissa spun around, searching for the speaker. At the door of a nearby cell stood the thin, bent figure of an old woman. Tangled gray hair fell to her shoulders, and a ragged tunic covered her body.

Alissa moved closer. "Why didn't you answer me when I called earlier?" she asked.

"I thought you might be a spy," replied the woman. "Sent by Mordock."

"And now?" asked Alissa.

"You destroyed his creature, didn't you? I guess you can be trusted. So, girl, what are you up to?"

"I've been looking for a friend," replied Alissa. "I found him in that cell," she added, pointing toward the end of the hall. "But I can't seem to wake him."

"Not likely you'll be able to," said the woman.

"What do you mean?" asked Alissa. Her voice shook as she continued, "He's not..." She couldn't go on.

The prisoner shook her head. "No, he's not dead. Though he may as well be, I fear."

"Why do you say that?" gulped Alissa.

"Because the old man's enchanted," replied the woman. "He's under Mordock's evil spell!"

CHAPTER EIGHT

Spells & Counterspells

lissa choked back a cry. A spell! She'd suspected as much.

"Do you know what kind of spell Mordock put him under?" she asked.

The woman's eyes darted about like those of a frightened animal. "No. But a powerful one, for sure. He's not said a word since Mordock brought him down here."

"Please, tell me everything," Alissa begged. "What did Mordock do? What did he say? Do you remember?"

The woman nervously twisted her hair. "Remember? If only I could forget! Mordock came down here with two of his guards. Carrying the old man like a sack of potatoes, they were. They dumped him on the floor." She shook her head, as if to rid it of the memory.

"What happened next?" prompted Alissa.

"Mordock stood over your friend, laughing like a madman. Frightened me, I'm not ashamed to admit. Then he began to talk. Low and cold like, yet so proud."

"What did he say?" asked Alissa once again.

"He said, 'You should have guarded your treasure more closely, old fool.' Not that I saw any treasure. I suppose Mordock must have already taken it. Whatever it was."

Alissa tried to be patient. "Did he say anything else?"

"Yes," replied the old woman. "Part of the spell it must have been. Mordock said, 'Enjoy your dreams, old friend. I'll make sure nothing disturbs you.' He muttered some strange words before he left."

The old woman shivered. "You can be sure I stayed out of sight. As I've done every time the sorcerer's come back."

Alissa felt a chill at the thought of Balin lying there help-lessly while Mordock watched him. She had to free him from this awful place. She had to!

Alissa stepped closer to the prisoner. "Thank you," she said gently. "I'm going to get my friend out of here. I'll do my best to see that you're freed too."

For a moment, hope flared in the woman's eyes. Just as rapidly, it died. "Don't be foolish, girl," she sighed. "There's nothing you can do. Not against one as powerful as Mordock." With that, she moved back into the darkness.

Alissa realized that the old woman would say nothing more. And she knew she must return to work before she was discovered near Balin's cell. So she picked up her nearly empty bucket, went back down the hall, and got busy.

As she scrubbed, Alissa wondered what treasure Mordock had spoken of. And what enchantment Balin was under.

"I must figure out how to break the spell," she murmured to herself. "Otherwise, what will we do? Even if Lia and I can escape from the castle, we can't carry Balin."

She continued to think—and scrub—until a guard came for her. Fortunately Gerda wasn't with him. Surely she would have noticed how little of the floor had been cleaned.

When she reached the kitchen, Alissa was surprised to see Lia there. Her friend was busy placing dishes on a huge tray.

"I hate to disturb your time in the dungeons," said Gerda.

"However, Lord Mordock's dinner must be prepared. So, clumsy as you are, you're needed here."

Gerda put Alissa to work polishing spoons and knives. Finally the silver gleamed to the housekeeper's satisfaction. "Take it to Lia," she ordered. "But don't touch that tray."

Alissa waited until the housekeeper moved away. Then she leaned close to her friend. "I found Balin!" she whispered.

Lia's head snapped up. She glanced nervously at Gerda before lowering her eyes to the tray again.

Alissa handed over the spoons and knives one by one. As Lia slowly set them on the tray, Alissa shared the story of her discovery. She ended with, "I have to get into that cell. And come up with a counterspell to wake Balin."

Gerda swept back into earshot before Lia could answer.

Alissa was next set to scrubbing potatoes. Before long, her thoughts began to drift. In her mind, she went through the pages of every book of spells she'd ever read. Surely she knew one that would work!

Bits and pieces came to her. But she couldn't remember any spells from beginning to end.

"Let's see," Alissa said under her breath. "Sand and saffron in water..." She shook her head. "No, that's not it!"

Words danced through her mind as she worked. Then it came to her! She whispered aloud:

> Ashes and saffron
> In a cup must steep
> With water and sugar
> To end a long sleep.

Alissa said the words to herself again and again. She didn't dare forget them.

The next time Gerda left the kitchen, Alissa shared her

news with Lia. "I've remembered a spell that might work," she whispered. She recited the words.

"How will we get the things we need?" asked Lia.

"We'll take them," said Alissa. "I've already got this."

She pulled something out of the bag at her waist. It was a burnt piece of wood with ashes flaking from its surface.

"I'll get the saffron," said Lia. "The spices are kept in Gerda's room. I have to go back in there to fetch the pitcher for Mordock's table."

"That just leaves the sugar," said Alissa. "And I see some right over there."

Lia looked where Alissa pointed. Sure enough, a dish filled with white grains sat on the table.

Alissa darted to the other side of the kitchen. Lia held her breath. There would be trouble if Gerda spotted the princess.

Several sets of curious eyes watched as Alissa picked up the dish. However, no one said a word. They simply studied her as she emptied half of the contents into a large white handkerchief. In seconds the handkerchief was knotted and safely hidden in Alissa's bag.

Footsteps sounded in the passageway. At once Alissa spun around and dashed back to the potatoes.

By the time Gerda returned, Alissa was madly scrubbing.

"You certainly haven't gotten far," complained the house-keeper. She added several more potatoes to Alissa's pile. "There'll be no dinner for you tonight if you don't get busy."

Alissa worked furiously for the next hour. Even Gerda could find no fault with her efforts. During that time, Lia was able to enter and exit Gerda's room. In answer to Alissa's raised eyebrows, Lia patted the bag at her waist.

At last the meal was ready. Mordock's dinner was carted

off to the study.

That meant it was the servants' turn. They lined up to receive their simple meal, then filed back to their cells.

While she ate, Alissa told Lia more of her adventures in the dungeon.

Lia shook her head in wonder. "And you're sure the spell you've remembered will wake Balin?" she asked.

Alissa swallowed and nodded. "I certainly hope so," she replied.

The girls set out the three ingredients—ashes, saffron, and sugar. The princess had saved some of her drinking water. Now she scooped up the ashes and dropped them into her cup.

"The saffron next, Lia," Alissa said. Lia sprinkled the spice into the cup. Then came the sugar. Alissa stirred until the mix was a runny paste. As she did, she recited the words of the spell.

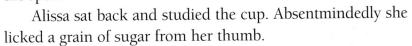

Alissa sat back and studied the cup. Absentmindedly she licked a grain of sugar from her thumb.

"Oh, toads' toenails!" she cried.

"What?" asked Lia.

"This isn't sugar," moaned Alissa. "It's salt! The spell will never work!"

Lia stared sadly at the runny mixture. "We can't try it again either," she said softly. "I took the last of the saffron."

CHAPTER NINE

A Familiar Face

he next morning, Alissa woke with a head filled with spells. However, they were all jumbled up in an impossible mess.

Lia's voice interrupted Alissa's troubled thoughts. "Have you remembered another spell that might wake Balin?"

"No," sighed Alissa. "And even if I had, it wouldn't be enough. I still haven't figured out how to get into his cell."

The door swung open, and the girls fell silent. Once more Gerda stood there, a guard at her side. The stern housekeeper shoved stale biscuits at them and marched off.

The rest of the morning went much like the one before. Lia disappeared upstairs. Alissa again found herself hard at work in the kitchen.

By midday, however, things changed. A frowning Gerda marched into the kitchen and up to Alissa. "Get a bucket of clean water!" she snapped.

More dark hallways to scrub, thought Alissa.

But to her surprise, Gerda announced, "You're to clean the floor in the study. And you're to do it quickly and quietly. His lordship will be working there."

The housekeeper moved off, mumbling under her breath. "The clumsiest scrub maid I've ever seen. Yet he makes a point of asking for her."

A sudden feeling of panic washed over Alissa. Had Mordock recognized her after all?

There was little time to wonder. In a matter of moments, she was in the sorcerer's study, scrubbing the floor. Mordock sat at a large table, sorting through the contents of a chest. From where she worked, Alissa couldn't see what was inside.

Not once did the sorcerer look at Alissa. His silence put Alissa on edge. If he was going to ignore her, why had he asked for her?

After a while, Alissa got up the courage to look around. Her eyes searched for something—anything—that might help her free Balin. When she spotted a shelf of bottles, she felt a rush of excitement. Surely they held magical ingredients! Unfortunately Mordock sat dangerously close by.

The princess worked her way around the room. When she was within a few feet of Mordock's table, he suddenly stood up. Alissa's heart leapt into her throat.

But the sorcerer didn't seem interested in her. Instead he shouted for his guards.

They answered his summons at once. "Take all of this now," Mordock ordered. "Put it with the rest of the treasure."

Upon hearing the word "treasure," Alissa's ears pricked up. Could the sorcerer be talking about the same treasure the old woman had heard him mention in the dungeon?

She lifted her head a bit. The guards were piling the chest high with coins and jewels. All probably stolen, she thought.

Mordock let out an angry shout. "Not that, you fool! Let me have it!"

Alissa raised her head a little higher. She saw Mordock snatch something from one of the guards.

She almost gasped when she saw what the sorcerer held.

It was a small carved wooden box—exactly like the one missing from Balin's tower! The one that the wizard had said must never leave Arcadia.

Alissa lowered her head before Mordock could notice her interest. She listened closely as he went on talking.

"I've told you," he snarled. "This box is never to leave my study. Never! Now get out of here!"

After the guards left, Mordock sank into his chair. "It's mine," he muttered angrily. "That weakling in the dungeon never dared use Narissa's gift. Not as it was meant to be used."

Narissa! Stunned, Alissa stopped scrubbing for a moment. She'd heard Balin speak the name with fondness. Many years ago, Narissa had given him lessons in wisdom and magic.

But what did Mordock have to do with Narissa? Perhaps he'd also been her student.

Mordock stroked the surface of the little box. "With this, no one can stop me. No one will have powers to equal mine."

Is it the box that's so magical or what's inside? Alissa wondered. Or both? Whichever it is, they can't be left in Mordock's hands. Their magic might free Balin.

Alissa rapidly scrubbed her way closer to the sorcerer. Maybe, just maybe, she could get a peek at what was in the carved box.

Bucket and brush in hand, the princess quietly rose to her feet. She tried to act like she was moving to another spot that needed scrubbing.

As she passed behind the wizard's chair, Alissa could see inside the box. There, resting on a cushion of dark blue velvet, was a tooth. A very large, very white tooth.

Alissa had never seen such a thing before. It must have belonged to a huge creature, she realized.

Alissa was so wrapped up in her thoughts that she forgot to be careful. Her bucket banged against Mordock's table.

At once the sorcerer slammed the box shut and pushed his chair back. One of the legs caught Alissa, and she tripped and fell. The bucket overturned, splashing her with cold, soapy water from head to shoulders.

Mordock laughed. "As bumbling as ever," he said, with a mocking smile. He turned his back on Alissa to place the carved box high on a nearby shelf.

"I'm sorry, my lord," sputtered Alissa, mopping up the mess as quickly as possible. The suds in her eyes made it hard to see. Without thinking, she wiped her face with a corner of her skirt. Along with the suds, she removed the dirt that had hidden her features.

When she looked at Mordock, she discovered that he was staring at her. "Stand up!" he ordered. He was no longer laughing.

Alissa slowly obeyed.

"Pull that wet hair away from your face," he continued. "And look at me!"

With trembling hands, Alissa did as she was told.

Mordock studied Alissa through narrowed eyes. "I've seen you before," he declared.

CHAPTER TEN

A Test of Magic

lissa felt as if her breath had been snatched away. Too late she realized her mistake. For the first time, Mordock could see her face clearly.

"I'm certain of it now. I've seen you somewhere before," Mordock repeated. "But where?" he murmured.

The sorcerer stepped nearer and took Alissa's chin in his hand. She tried not to shiver at his touch.

"P-p-perhaps you saw me at the village fair, my lord," she stammered.

Mordock dropped his hand. "I think not," he said in his frostiest voice.

Alissa gave the sorcerer a curtsy. "I'll leave you now, sir," Picking up bucket and brush, she darted toward the door.

"STAY!" thundered Mordock.

Alissa halted, her back to the sorcerer.

"Turn around, girl," he ordered. "Look at me."

The princess faced Mordock once again. As she watched, he raised his hands high in the air. A string of strange words poured from his lips. And suddenly a round object appeared in his cupped hands. It seemed to be a huge soap bubble— shimmering and shaking in the candlelight. Colors reflected from its surface and danced on the stone walls. Then the bubble slowly grew smaller and became solid.

When Mordock lowered his hands, he held a silvery ball. "Now we shall discover where I've seen you," he said with a satisfied nod. "And who you are." He studied the ball's shiny surface.

Alissa thought about running, but she knew it would do no good. Where could she flee that Mordock wouldn't find her? She closed her eyes, waiting for Mordock's rage to explode.

"Cursed ball!" the sorcerer roared. "It shows me nothing!"

Alissa's eyes popped open. Mordock was angry, that was clear. However, his anger didn't seem to be directed at her.

With another shout, the sorcerer threw the silvery globe into the air. He clapped his hands and the ball burst into flames. In an instant, only a puff of smoke remained.

Mordock's black eyes drilled into Alissa. "Don't think this ends it," he hissed. "I will find out who you are. You can't block my powers forever, you know. Do you have any idea how powerful I am?"

Alissa had no answer to the sorcerer's question. But she had a horrible feeling that soon both of them would find out.

"Now leave me!" snarled Mordock.

Alissa turned and ran from the room. She didn't stop until she was halfway down the hall. Then she leaned against the wall, trying to calm herself.

Alissa finally found the strength to move again. As she headed back to the kitchen, she sorted through her confused thoughts. Why had Mordock's powers failed him? Was he a fake after all?

But she knew that wasn't so. She'd seen the sorcerer's

powers at work. They were real enough.

Then a thought struck her. Perhaps she was under a spell. One cast by Balin to protect her.

Her hand went to the locket hidden under her dress. This must be why Balin had warned her not to take it off. Somehow it must block Mordock's powers.

She remembered that she'd thought about removing the locket to hide it. Thank goodness Lia had reminded her of Balin's words!

Alissa made her way back into the kitchen, hoping that Gerda hadn't heard the shouting from Mordock's study. And it seemed that the housekeeper hadn't. She merely nodded at the sight of Alissa and pointed to a heap of dirty pots. "Get busy with those."

Alissa obeyed without a murmur. She didn't dare talk to Lia, who was making bread nearby.

As the day crawled on, Alissa tried to keep her mind on two things. The first was Balin's box. The wizard had told her that it should never leave Arcadia. And when it did, terrible things had begun happening. She had to find a way to get the box out of Mordock's study.

Alissa also thought about a spell that would open locks. She searched her memory for something that might work.

Then it came to her. Of course! It was such a simple spell. All she needed was—

Suddenly a chill fell over the room. Puzzled, Alissa looked toward the arched doorway. Mordock stood there, his arms folded across his chest. His cold eyes searched the kitchen.

For a moment, Alissa's hands stopped moving. Then she forced herself to go on with her work. From under her lashes, she watched as Gerda hurried toward the sorcerer.

"Really, your lordship. You hardly need to come to the kitchen. Just send someone for me, and I'll see that—"

A sharp motion of Mordock's hand silenced the house-keeper. Without speaking, he entered the room.

Alissa kept her head down, hoping that she was wrong. Perhaps the sorcerer wasn't here because of her.

That hope died when a shadow fell across the table. Alissa raised her head and met Mordock's mocking glance.

Gerda hurried to the sorcerer's side. "Has this miserable serving girl offended you, my lord?" she asked.

Mordock took his time answering. "Hardly. Not this one." He moved around the table toward Alissa. "In fact, I find her interesting. She's not the usual prisoner, you see."

The sorcerer stopped right in front of Alissa. There was no mistaking the challenge in his eyes.

Then, without a word to Alissa, he spun about and marched out of the room. At the door, he paused only to shout Gerda's name.

Alissa stood where she was, shaking from head to foot. Several captives glanced at her curiously, though no one spoke. Only Lia looked at Alissa directly—her green eyes filled with worry.

All too soon, Gerda was back. She approached Alissa, a frown on her face. "I don't know what's going on here. No matter what Lord Mordock says, it's easy to see that you've upset him. Yet he requests that you serve him his dinner tomorrow."

Alissa swallowed hard. So the battle would continue another day.

CHAPTER ELEVEN

Tricking a Sorcerer

ome in," ordered Mordock.

Alissa took a deep breath. Tightening her hold on the dinner tray, she entered Mordock's study for the second time.

All last night and today she'd been thinking about this meeting. She and Lia had visited Crispin's cell again. They'd told him about the carved box that Alissa wanted to sneak out of the sorcerer's study.

Together, the three of them had come up with a plan. Now it was up to Alissa to carry it out.

When he caught sight of Alissa, Mordock's lips curved slightly. "I hardly recognize you in that outfit, girl. But don't worry," he added with a smile. "I will."

The clean blouse and vest had been Gerda's idea. The housekeeper felt it wasn't proper to serve "his lordship" in rags.

Now Alissa set out dishes. As she did so, she searched for Balin's box. She spotted it at the table's edge amid a pile of books. The lid was up, and the tooth gleamed against the dark velvet. Almost within reach, Alissa told herself.

She finished laying out the meal and stepped back.

The sorcerer ate without hurry. His eyes kept wandering to Alissa. Each time they did, a smile passed over his face.

At last Mordock sat back. "A most satisfactory meal," he declared. "You may tell Gerda I said so."

Alissa hesitated. Is he going to let me go? she wondered.

Mordock seemed to read her mind. "You seem concerned, Alissa. Afraid that I may guess your secret?"

"How would I dare to have secrets from one with such power?" murmured Alissa.

"A good question," replied Mordock. "For the longer you keep secrets from me, the worse your fate will be."

With that, the sorcerer waved toward the table. "Clean this up," he ordered. "I will expect to see you again tomorrow night." He added with a smile, "The night after that too. In fact, for as long as it takes."

Mordock leaned forward. "Perhaps your friend should join us. What is her name? Lia? Maybe with her here, your memory will improve."

Alissa felt a touch of fear. Would her locket protect Lia as well? But her fear was soon replaced by a cold anger. Now, she told herself. Now is my chance.

Alissa moved forward to clean up the table. Silverware, pitcher, dishes—all went on the tray.

Suddenly a heavy plate shot out of her hand. At the same time, she dropped a napkin on the table.

But Mordock didn't notice the napkin. His eyes followed the silver plate as it fell and began rolling about on the floor.

By the time Mordock turned back toward her, Alissa was bending down to snatch up the plate. She quickly added it to the pile of dishes.

"Ah, Alissa," said the sorcerer. "You're amusing, if nothing else. Though we both know you *are* something else."

Alissa kept her head down. Grabbing the napkin with both hands, she placed that on the tray too. Then she lifted the heavy load and prepared to go. But Mordock's hand came down on her arm, forcing her to lower the tray.

"I think you've made a mistake," he said in an icy voice.

Alissa froze as Mordock lifted the napkin. "Surely you didn't mean to take *this* back to the kitchen," he said. He pulled Balin's box from the pile of dishes.

"Oh no, my lord," protested Alissa. "Of course not."

Mordock held the box in his hands for a moment, his eyes burning into Alissa's. More than anything, the princess longed to escape from his unblinking gaze. But she managed to stare back at him steadily.

Finally he waved her away. "Go!" he ordered. "And try not to be so careless tomorrow."

The sorcerer was placing the box on the shelf as Alissa backed from the room. Once out the door, she fled down the hall. She was almost to the kitchen before she stopped waiting for Mordock to call her back.

~~

Dressed in her old clothes again, Alissa went to her cell for the night. Lia was there, eyes wide with questions.

Alissa held a finger to her lips and Lia nodded. They ate in silence until the guard's footsteps faded into the distance.

"Did you get the box?" whispered Lia.

The princess shook her head. "No," she replied. "I had it on the tray under a napkin. Then Mordock noticed. For a minute, I was afraid he knew what I was up to."

"Oh, Alissa," shuddered Lia.

"Don't worry, I did get something." Alissa reached into her pocket and pulled out the great tooth.

She sighed as she studied it. "I don't know if it's the tooth or the box that holds the power. But this is all I could get."

"How did you ever manage that much?" asked Lia.

Alissa laughed. "I thought about what Mordock did when we saw him in Arcadia," she replied. "Remember his tricks?"

"Of course. How he made things appear and disappear. Wasn't it magic?"

Alissa shook her head. "I asked Balin. He said it wasn't really magic. Mordock just made us look somewhere else."

"So you did the same thing?" asked Lia.

"Yes. When I was picking up Mordock's dishes, I dropped a plate on purpose. While he was watching it, I slipped the tooth out of the box. By the time he looked back, the tooth was in my pocket. And the box was under the napkin!"

"It's a good thing he didn't check inside the box when he took it back," noted Lia. "Although..."

Alissa shivered. "I know. He's bound to do that sooner or later. That means we'd better carry out the rest of our plan tonight."

So the chill hour before dawn found the girls standing by their door. They were waiting for the guard to go by as he made his rounds.

"Here he comes," whispered Lia. They listened to the guard march past.

As soon as the hall was clear, the girls set off. In minutes they were safely inside Crispin's chamber.

"Are you ready?" asked the boy.

"We're ready," said Alissa. "And Crispin…"

He looked at her expectantly.

"Thank you," Alissa said softly. "I promise we'll try to get you and the others out of here too."

Crispin gave her his usual carefree grin. "That would save me some work," he said. "But it's not the real reason I'm helping. There's nothing I'd like better than to see you beat Mordock at his own game."

They crept into the hall and tiptoed to the end of the passage. There they waited, hardly breathing, until the guard's footsteps sounded behind them.

"He's almost here," whispered Crispin. "Get moving. Remember, don't stop for anything."

Alissa and Lia nodded and darted off.

Behind them, the footsteps came closer. Then, in a voice loud enough to wake the entire castle, Crispin cried, "You'll never catch us!"

CHAPTER TWELVE

Tight Corners & Dead Ends

Alissa and Lia sped down the narrow passage. They could still hear Crispin's excited shouts. His voice was sometimes high and sometimes low. It sounded like every captive in the castle had broken loose at the same time.

Under cover of the noise, the girls raced in the opposite direction. They knew Crispin would lead the guard away from them. Alissa tried to think only about making her way through the twisting passages. She had to remember how she'd reached the dungeons before!

She made one wrong turn but soon corrected her mistake. Pulling Lia along with her, Alissa dashed madly toward the steep stairway that led to the dungeon. Down the stone steps they flew.

At the bottom, the girls paused and listened. There was no sign that anyone was following them.

"This is it," said Alissa. "If ever I've needed a spell to work, it's now. If we can't get into Balin's cell, we'll never be able to free him."

She slipped from her pocket the only ingredient needed for this spell. The one thing she'd had close to hand all the time she was scrubbing floors and pots: soap.

Alissa smeared the soap on the lock that held the outside

door of the dungeon closed. Shutting her eyes, she recited the words to the spell she'd remembered.

No lock, no chain,
No bars, no rope
Will block the way
If rubbed with soap.

"Look!" cried Lia.

Alissa slowly opened her eyes. Drops of sizzling metal were striking the floor. The lock was melting! She yanked at the door, and the lock snapped.

The girls charged through the cold dungeons to the last cell. Quickly Alissa smeared more soap and chanted the words of the spell. The first door opened, as did the second.

Now only one lock separated them from Balin.

Then Lia glanced behind them. "The guards are coming!"

"No!" moaned Alissa.

There wasn't time to melt another lock. Alissa stretched out her arm toward the motionless Balin. If she could get to him, maybe she could break the spell.

Suddenly an idea struck her. Even if she couldn't touch Balin, perhaps the tooth could!

At that moment, the guards rounded the corner. Without a word, Lia placed herself between them and Alissa.

The princess stuck her hand between the bars and threw the tooth. It sailed through the air, tumbling and turning. Alissa held her breath. If this didn't work, they were lost.

The tooth dropped—right on Balin's robe! Immediately the wizard stirred. His eyes fluttered, and he reached up to grab the tooth. Once his fingers closed around it, he was fully awake. He sat up with a jerk.

Balin turned to the door just as the first guard reached Lia. As she struggled, a second guard pushed past her and seized Alissa.

"Alissa? Lia?" the wizard said, his voice cracking. He staggered to his feet and moved toward the barred door.

The guards' blank eyes fixed on the old wizard. It was impossible to tell what thoughts were passing through their minds—if any. But they seemed to come to a decision. They ignored Balin and began dragging their captives off.

Alissa twisted around to take one last look through the barred door. I failed, she thought. The tooth woke Balin. But he's still too weak to free himself.

As she watched, Balin lifted one shaky arm. She could see the gleam of the tooth in his hand. To her amazement, the bars of the cell door faded in a cloud of yellow smoke.

"Stop!" shouted the wizard.

The guards whirled around. At the sight of Balin standing free, they let go of the girls. Holding their spears before them, the guards blocked the passage.

Balin advanced down the hall. Again he raised the tooth. This time the guards' spears began to steam. In seconds those too had become a smoky mist.

The guards stared at their empty hands. Then they turned and ran.

As the guards made their escape, the wizard leaned against the wall. Alissa and Lia rushed toward him.

"Are you all right?" asked Alissa.

"What are you doing here?" Balin asked in a faint voice.

"Bartok brought us to you," replied Alissa.

Balin nodded, then opened his hand. He studied the tooth

as if seeing it for the first time.

"Where did you get this?" he murmured.

"Mordock had it," Alissa replied. "But I couldn't get the box. Does it matter?"

Balin laughed softly. "No, Alissa. This holds the power," he said, staring down at the treasure. "The dragon's tooth."

"It's from a real dragon!" exclaimed Alissa. Though her mind buzzed with questions, she knew this wasn't the time to ask. "Balin, we've got to get out of here. Mordock is going to be looking for the tooth. And for us."

"I'm ready," said the wizard. Yet Alissa and Lia could see that he was far from his powerful self. Alissa put an arm around Balin's waist to support him. Then they all started down the hall.

As they passed the next cell, Alissa glimpsed a figure. It was the old woman, the one who'd told her about Balin.

"Balin, we must help—" Alissa began.

The woman stopped her. "You can see he's weak as a babe. Get him out of here. That's what matters now."

Balin nodded once in the woman's direction. Their eyes held, and she smiled. "Go safely," she said.

The three moved as rapidly as they could. At the top of the dungeon steps, they stopped to give Balin time to rest.

Lia checked the long passage. "I don't hear any other guards," she whispered.

"Do you suppose they captured Crispin?" asked Alissa.

"So you've had some help," Balin noted.

"Yes," replied Alissa. "From a very brave friend."

Balin read her mind. "We will be back to free him, Alissa. And the others. But first we must save ourselves—and defeat Mordock. Otherwise, there's no way we can help anyone."

Alissa knew that Balin was right. "We'd better head for the drawbridge," she suggested. "That's the only way out of here." She gave Balin a worried glance. "The bridge is probably raised. And I have no idea how to lower it."

"Remember, I have the tooth now," said Balin. "Get us there, and leave the rest to me."

Alissa led the way through the halls. To her relief, she saw no guards. They all must have been searching for Crispin.

The three rounded the last corner. Ahead of them towered the huge drawbridge.

But here their luck ran out. Armor clattered behind them, and they spun around to see a dozen guards headed their way!

Both girls looked toward Balin. The wizard stood directly before the drawbridge, his eyes closed. He clutched the tooth tightly in his wrinkled hands.

"Hurry, Balin!" begged Alissa.

The wizard's eyes remained closed. He was saying something over and over under his breath.

Suddenly the drawbridge groaned, creaked, and began to lower. Through the opening, Alissa caught sight of the morning sky. But the guards were nearly upon them.

Balin dropped his hands. "Run!" he cried. "We can't wait for it to go all the way down."

The girls didn't need to be told twice. They scrambled up the steep slope of the bridge and raced to the end.

Here they were forced to stop. They could see the moat's edge both ahead of and below them. A broad strip of muddy water separated them from dry ground. As they nervously eyed the gap, they spotted fins in the water below.

The first of the guards stepped onto the bridge. Then Mordock himself appeared. With an angry shout, the sorcerer

lifted his arms. As though he'd pulled a string, the bridge jerked to a stop. A moment later, it began to rise back toward the castle.

"We'll have to jump!" shouted Balin. "Before it's too late."

He grabbed Alissa with one hand and Lia with the other. He didn't give them time to think. He simply yelled, "Now!"

They sailed through the air. Alissa held her breath, waiting to feel the dark waters close over her head.

Suddenly she felt hard earth beneath her. A disappointed monster snapped at her heels, narrowly missing its target.

Alissa dragged herself to her feet. To her relief, she saw that Lia was helping the wizard get up.

"To the forest," Balin panted.

The three sped across the clearing and into the forest. They'd hadn't gone far when a squawk sounded overhead.

"Bartok!" cried Balin joyfully. The bird settled on the old wizard's shoulder with another squawk.

"Come!" ordered Balin. "We must get away from here!"

They'd only gone a few feet when a blinding flash struck just in front of them. Lightning! They ducked as another bolt followed—and a third.

Finally they dared to stand up again. But then they caught sight of what the lightning had created. A wall of thick, twisted vines had grown up in front of them, blocking their way.

And behind them marched a troop of empty-eyed guards—with Mordock in the lead.

CHAPTER THIRTEEN

Balin's Battle

lissa spun wildly around, searching for a way to escape. But there was nowhere to go.

"Balin," she said, her voice trembling.

The wizard laid a gentle hand on her arm. "It's all right."

Balin stepped forward to meet his enemy. For a moment, a look of confusion crossed Mordock's face. Then he smiled and signaled his guards to wait.

"So you've made your escape?" Mordock mocked. "How clever of you! And what have you to show for all your efforts?"

Balin's answer was calm and steady. "What do I have to show? This, Mordock." He opened his hand.

"The tooth!" screamed the sorcerer. "You can't have taken that from me!"

In two steps, Balin was back at the wall of vines. Using the tooth, he sliced through the vines with one strong stroke. The wall shook and crumbled to the ground.

But Mordock wasn't about to let his old enemy get away. He raised his hands, and a blast of icy wind knocked Balin and the two girls off their feet. Bartok tumbled through the air, squawking in fear.

"Tooth or no tooth, you're still weak, old man!" Mordock shouted. "Even weaker than when I defeated you earlier."

Alissa and Lia struggled to their feet. Balin had only made it as far as his knees. Yet when the girls started toward him, the wizard motioned them away.

Mordock stopped not ten feet from Balin. He ignored Alissa and Lia. His rage was all directed toward the wizard.

"What a fool you are!" he hissed in a hate-filled voice. "You could have used the power of the tooth. Instead you kept it hidden away. Safe in its little box in your tower. As dear Narissa would have wished it."

The sorcerer circled the wizard, his back to Alissa and Lia. Balin sharply ordered the girls, "Both of you go! Now!"

However, neither Alissa nor Lia moved. They weren't about to leave Balin.

Mordock continued to close in on the wizard. Why isn't Balin getting up? thought Alissa fearfully. Then she noticed that the wizard's hand was empty. He'd dropped the tooth when he fell! It lay on the ground between the wizard and the sorcerer.

Slowly Balin's hand stretched toward the tooth. But Mordock saw. He shouted the words of a spell, and at once a terrible pain seized Balin. The wizard gasped and his hand fell useless to his side.

"No!" Lia whispered in horror. Without the tooth, Balin was too weak to fight back. Mordock had won.

Suddenly Alissa remembered. The tooth wasn't the only thing with magical powers. There was Balin's locket as well. It had shielded the princess against all of Mordock's attempts to identify her.

With one sharp tug, Alissa freed the locket from her neck. She pressed it into Lia's hand, whispering, "Take it to Balin."

Now I must give Lia her chance, Alissa thought. She

edged farther away from the fallen wizard. Then she stopped. "Mordock!" she shouted.

The sorcerer spun to face her, his eyes alight with victory. For a moment, he stared at Alissa in wonder. Then he crowed, "At last! Whatever enchantment you were under is ended! I know who you are! The princess of Arcadia!"

A deep frown wrinkled his forehead. "You caused me a great deal of trouble when we met in your kingdom," he declared. "It will be my pleasure to return the favor now that we're in mine."

While Mordock's attention was on Alissa, Lia darted to Balin's side. Quickly she slipped the locket into his hands. Almost at once, Balin stirred. Color flowed back into his drained face, and his eyes began to glow. He rose to his feet, all signs of weakness erased.

I was right, thought Alissa. The locket will protect Balin from Mordock's power. Just as it protected me.

She began to back away, her eyes fixed on the sorcerer. Mordock gave an evil smile and moved to close the gap between them.

"Really, princess. There's nowhere left to run," Mordock observed. "At the rate you're going, you'll soon be right in the arms of my guards."

Behind Mordock, Balin stepped forward. "I suggest you take care of me first."

The sorcerer whirled around, disbelief on his face. Balin faced him, tall and sure.

"After all, you've been waiting for this moment for ages," continued the wizard. His voice rang out strong and clear. "In fact, since the day Narissa gave us our first lesson in magic you've hated me. Secretly at first. Then so openly that even she couldn't forgive you."

"I have no need for forgiveness," Mordock shot back.

Balin ignored the interruption. His eyes blazing, he said, "Narissa gave the tooth to me because she knew you couldn't be trusted. I promised to use its powers wisely—and to keep it out of your grasp."

"See how well you've managed that," mocked Mordock. "Fool! You haven't the wisdom or strength to defend yourself. You certainly can't defend the tooth—or your little helpers."

He lifted his arm, pointing past Balin and toward Lia, who was reaching for the dragon's tooth. Mordock's magic brought her to her knees with a cry of pain.

"It's my helpers who have saved me," declared Balin. So saying, he raised the locket and held it in front of his chest.

Mordock threw up his arms, ready to cast another spell. Balin stood his ground, lifting the locket high over his head.

It was as though the locket summoned the sun itself. For at once, an early-morning sunbeam cut through the trees to strike it. A burst of rainbow colors lit the wizard's face. The light grew, surrounding Mordock and his men.

Then the light began to spin. Trees swayed and bent as the glowing circle created its own howling wind. And over the sound of the wind could be heard a high-pitched humming noise. It sounded like someone was rubbing a finger along the rim of an enormous glass.

The light was so bright that it took Alissa a moment to realize that it was also narrowing. And it was becoming even brighter and faster.

With a ringing echo, as if the giant glass were shattering, the circle of light broke apart. Bright bits of color rained over the trees and fell to the ground. The last tiny pieces vanished into the grass.

All was silent. Mordock and his guards were gone.

Alissa took a deep breath. On shaky legs, she hurried to her friends. "Balin! Lia!" she cried. "Are you all right?"

Lia could only nod, too stunned for words. But Balin held out a hand to Alissa. "Yes," he told her. "Thanks to you."

Lia bent down to pick up the white tooth. Gently she laid it in the wizard's palm. He smiled his thanks.

It was Alissa who first noted the change behind them. "The castle!" she exclaimed.

Grimrock still stood in the middle of the clearing. Yet it was completely changed. Now it was a tumbled-down pile of pale-gray stone, covered with ivy. And in place of the dark moat, there ran a circle of sparkling blue water.

"Mordock's spell on the old castle has been broken too," Alissa said. "Grimrock is gone."

"What about the other prisoners?" whispered Lia.

As if in response, people began to stream out from behind the heaps of stone. Leading them was Crispin!

Alissa and Lia ran toward the group. Noisy greetings filled the clearing. Finally Alissa asked, "What happened to Gerda?"

"It was strange," said Crispin with a laugh. "She and a pair of guards were about to haul me off to the dungeons. All at once, Gerda screamed and vanished in a burst of smoke. I looked around, and the guards were gone as well."

When the excitement died down, Alissa introduced Balin to Crispin.

"I thank you for your bravery," the wizard told the boy.

"Mostly it's Alissa and Lia you should thank," replied Crispin. "And so should we."

The former captives said their good-byes. They were eager to reach their homes and loved ones. But before heading into the trees, Crispin turned back. "If you're ever back this way, I'm at your service!" he called. With a lighthearted wave, he disappeared.

Soon the clearing was quiet again. As Alissa studied the ruins, she shook her head. It was hard to believe a great castle had stood on the spot just moments before.

She smiled at her friends. "Time we went home too."

"Yes," said Balin. "And I don't plan to leave Arcadia again for a good long while."

The three tired travelers made their way along the forest path. As they walked, Alissa's questions tumbled out. There was so much she still didn't understand. Why had Balin never told her about the dragon's tooth? Or the locket? Could she learn to use their powers herself?

Balin sighed. "Remember, Alissa: With great power comes great responsibility." He continued, "It's not enough to possess power. You must also know when and how to use it."

Alissa slowly nodded. "Father says much the same thing about being king."

"I trust your father to use his powers wisely. As I trust you will do when you're queen," said Balin.

"And as Narissa trusted you," Lia added.

"She did," the wizard said. "Though I don't look forward to the day when I'll have to use those powers again."

"But Mordock is gone," said Alissa.

"For now," said Balin. "I haven't completely destroyed

him, Alissa. I can't do that."

"So we must be ready for him. Always," said Alissa softly.

Balin nodded. For a time, they walked on in silence. They were thinking about the battle they'd just faced—and the ones still to come.

It was midday when they heard it—the sound of hoof-beats pounding through the forest.

"Someone's coming!" Alissa cried. "We'd better hide!"

Balin smiled. "No need," he said. "They're friends."

A dozen mounted soldiers charged through the trees. And leading them was—

"Father!" cried Alissa. She ran forward, with Lia at her heels.

King Edmund leapt from his horse and folded both girls into his arms.

"Alissa...Lia..." he murmured. "Thank the stars that you're both all right. We've been hunting for you for days. But we couldn't make our way into this strange forest. Walls of trees and vines seemed to grow up before our very eyes. Until this morning, that is. Then a clear path suddenly appeared through the woods."

Alissa glanced at her father's soldiers, who stood several yards away. It was quite a rescue party for two girls and an old wizard. Though only King Edmund would have known that the friend who needed rescuing was Balin.

Alissa quietly told her father about her adventure. When she finished, she realized that she wasn't sure how to explain Balin to the soldiers. The old wizard had always insisted on keeping his presence in Arcadia a secret.

She searched for Balin. But he—and Bartok—were nowhere to be seen.

"Father! Lia!" she whispered. "Balin's gone!"

King Edmund didn't seem surprised by the news. "Don't worry, Alissa. He'll be waiting for you in his tower."

Alissa nodded in relief. Of course he would. The wizard still had many things to teach her. Many tasks to give her too. In fact, she wasn't sure she'd remembered to clean Balin's old iron pot before she left.

Alissa smiled. She found that for once she was actually looking forward to the job.

More to Explore

Have fun exploring more about both the simple and spectacular treasures that you might find in a medieval castle. And there are great projects for you to do too!

Treasure Box

Balin kept the dragon's tooth in a special box. You can make a box and use it to store a treasure of your own.

What you need

- Ruler
- 5" x 8" index card
- Pencil with eraser
- Scissors
- 9" x 12" poster paper
- Clear tape
- Materials for decorating. Use markers, crayons, stickers, artificial jewels, glitter, wrapping paper, tin foil, buttons, sewing trims, ribbons, small artificial flowers—anything you want.

What you do

1. Make patterns for the box parts. Use the ruler to make three rectangles on the index card, as shown on page 87. Rectangle A is 5" x 2½". Rectangle B is 5" x 1½". Rectangle C is 2½" x 1½". Be sure your measurements are exact.

2. Label the rectangles as shown and cut them out.

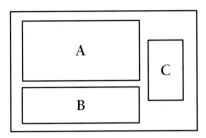

Steps 1 and 2

3. On poster board, use the patterns to outline the shape shown at the right. You will be tracing each pattern piece twice. (Do not write the letters on your shape.)

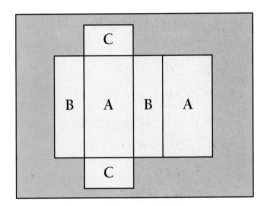

Step 3

4. Draw tabs as shown at the right.

5. Cut along the outside edges of the shape. Do NOT cut along any of the inside lines. These are fold lines. And be careful not to cut the tabs off.

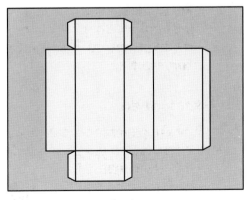

Step 4

87

6. Lay the shape out on a flat surface with the pencil lines down. Fold up along one of the pencil lines, being careful to fold a straight line. Use your fingernails or the edge of the ruler to crease the fold. Then lay the folded section flat again.

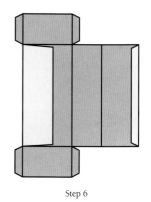

Step 6

7. Continue until you have folded along each of the pencil lines, including those on the flaps.

8. Turn the shape over and lay it out flat. Carefully erase the pencil lines.

9. Think about how you want to decorate the box. If you're going to draw your designs, do that before you assemble the box. Remember which part is the bottom and which is the lid. That may affect your design. If you want to use materials that you will glue or stick to the box, assemble the box before you decorate it.

10. Turn the shape over again. Working with one corner at a time, tape the side flaps to the inside of the box.

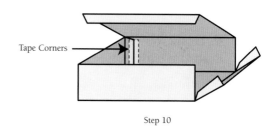

Tape Corners

Step 10

11. Fold the lid down and tuck the flap inside.

12. Decorate your box if you haven't already done so.

13. You may want to use velvet or another fancy cloth to line your box. Just cut a 2½" x 5" rectangle of cloth and glue it to the inside bottom of the box.

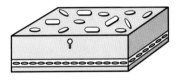

Windowsill Herb Garden

Herbs and spices were extremely important in medieval times. They were used not only in cooking but for medicine.

Most spices grow in tropical areas, so they had to be imported. But every castle had its own herb garden. You can too. In fact, you can grow herbs indoors, right on a sunny windowsill.

What you need

- Several sections of old newspaper
- A small container for each type of seed. Use clay pots, peat pots, or plastic drink cups.
- Gravel or several small rocks
- Commercial potting soil
- Three or four kinds of herb seeds (See page 91 for a list of herbs you can grow.)
- Marker
- Masking tape
- Long, shallow dish or rimmed tray that will fit on a windowsill and hold the pots
- Water

Knotty Gardens

Medieval gardeners liked to plant their herbal gardens in colorful patterns. Favorite patterns were checkerboards, wheels, and lacy loops or "knots."

What you do

1. Place the newspaper on your work surface. Set the pots on the newspaper.

2. Put some gravel or a small rock in the bottom of each pot.

3. Fill the pots with potting soil, stopping about 1" from the rim.

4. Sprinkle seeds lightly over the surface of the soil—one type of seed for each pot.

5. Cover the seeds with a small amount of potting soil.

6. Use the marker and strips of masking tape to label each pot of herbs.

7. Put the shallow dish or tray in a sunny spot on the windowsill. Line the pots up in this container.

8. Sprinkle about ⅛ cup of water over each pot. Be sure to water whenever the soil gets dry. But don't soak your herbs!

9. When your herbs have grown, use scissors to harvest them. See the suggestions on page 92 for some ideas about how to use your herbs.

Herbs you can grow

- Basil
- Chives
- Mint
- Oregano
- Parsley
- Rosemary
- Thyme

Medicine Chest

In medieval times, herbs were used to treat many illnesses. Saffron was thought to ease colic—cramps that babies often have. Anise and cumin were used to cure stomachaches. Mint, parsley, and chives were supposed to increase energy and well-being. A wound might be cleaned with garlic or rosemary boiled in water.

Today scientists believe that some of these old herbal remedies are actually helpful. In fact, there are businesses that sell nothing but medicinal herbs.

Use your herbs

- Dress up your dinner plate with a sprig of parsley. (It also makes a good breath freshener.)

- Add a few mint leaves to a cup of tea or hot chocolate.

- Sprinkle rosemary and thyme on baked chicken.

- Crumble some dried basil leaves and add them to your favorite spaghetti sauce.

- Chop some chives and sprinkle them on cottage cheese or potatoes.

> ### Colorful Additions
> Medieval cooks used herbs and spices not only to appeal to the taste but to the eye. Red was a popular color for food, especially in winter. For instance, the spice sandalwood was added to turn gingerbread red. Other favorite food colors were purple, white, green, yellow, and black. On special occasions, a cook might turn out a meat pie that combined layers of these colors.

- Dry your oregano and use it on top of a slice of pizza.

- Cut some long stems of herbs. Hang them upside down in a cool, dark place until they are dry. Then add a ribbon and put them in a vase as a dried herb bouquet.

Make Your Own Magic

Try some wizardry of your own with this amazing paper clip magic trick.

What you need

- Strip of paper (approximately 1" x 10")
- Two small paper clips

What you do

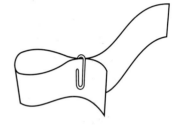

1. Hold the strip of paper in both hands and curve one end around as shown. Attach a paper clip with the short section on the outside.

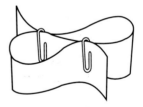

2. Curve the other end of the strip around to the back. Paper clip it as shown, being sure the short section of the clip faces the inside of the curve.

3. Hold one end of the strip in each hand. Recite some magic words as you pull on both ends at the same time. The paper clips will fly off the strip—and they will be hooked together!

Important: Practice this trick several times before trying it in front of a friend. Pull slowly until you get the hang of the trick. Pull quickly when you demonstrate the trick.

Stardust Story Sampler

Stardust Classics books feature other heroines to believe in. Come explore with Laurel the Woodfairy and Kat the Time Explorer. Here are short selections from their books.

Selection from

LAUREL RESCUES THE PIXIES

Laurel fluttered along the path, with her friend Ivy close behind.

"Oh, Laurel," Ivy gasped. "You're not really going to go and stay with the pixies, are you?"

"Yes, I am," said Laurel. "I just don't fit in here. Besides, the Eldest thinks it's a good idea. And so do I."

"Well, I don't," said Ivy. "I'm sure the Eldest would understand if you changed your mind."

By now they could hear the roar of Thunder Falls. Soon the falls and pond came into sight. Laurel flitted to a huge oak tree that grew near the waterfall. Her sunlit treehouse was nestled in the branches high above.

Laurel ignored the ladder and flew up to the porch. Ivy followed, still trying to think of a way to get her friend to stay.

Once inside, Laurel gazed around a bit sadly. She really couldn't imagine leaving her lovely home forever.

Still, she'd made up her mind to go. So that was exactly what she was going to do!

With a sigh, Laurel gathered up her traveling bag and began packing. She threw in some clean dresses and extra pairs of slippers.

"You're certainly packing a lot of things," noted Ivy. She'd been pacing the floor in silence while Laurel got ready.

"I may be gone a long time," replied Laurel.

"Oh, Laurel," moaned Ivy. "I'm afraid I'll never see you again."

"Don't worry," said Laurel, giving her friend a hug. "I'll be back. Even if I decide to stay with the pixies forever, I'll come to visit you."

"Stay forever?" exclaimed Ivy. "Please, Laurel! Don't even think that way! This is just supposed to be a visit."

"A visit!" echoed a familiar voice. "Why, you must be talking about me."

Laurel and Ivy whirled around. Outside on the porch stood Foxglove, a wide smile on his face.

The pixie smoothed down his shaggy black hair and straightened his fishskin tunic. "Sorry. I didn't mean to listen in like that," he said. "But it's hot out in the forest today. I was in a hurry to get up here where there's a breeze. So I came scrambling up the ladder without even a hello."

Laurel waved him inside. "You're always welcome. You know that."

As Foxglove stepped forward, his bright eyes lit on Laurel's traveling bag. "You're all ready for an adventure," he remarked. "I didn't know we had one planned!"

"I'm going away for a while," said Laurel.

Foxglove studied her face, noting that she seemed more sad than excited. "Going away?" he echoed. He glanced at Ivy, who only shook her head.

The pixie turned back to Laurel. "Would you like some company?" he asked with a smile.

"Well, actually, I'd *be* the company," Laurel said. "I

thought I'd come to stay with the pixies for a while. In your village."

Foxglove's smile suddenly disappeared.

Laurel felt her heart sink. Foxglove certainly didn't act happy about taking her home with him. Maybe he didn't want her around either.

Maybe she wasn't welcome anywhere!

Selection from
KAT AND THE SECRETS OF THE NILE

Kat and Jessie moved closer to the riverbank. Fine ladies stood on the deck of a tour boat. They wore lovely long gowns and shaded themselves with parasols. On the bank below, barefoot children jumped up and down, begging for coins. Meanwhile, gentlemen in handsome dark suits stood on the dock. Some shouted orders to robed workers.

For a moment, Kat and Jessie watched. Then Kat turned to her aunt. "I know how to find out exactly where we are and what year it is," she said. "See? That man is reading a newspaper. It's bound to have the date on it somewhere."

Kat wandered nearer to the man with the newspaper. As she passed him, she pretended to trip.

"Careful, miss," said the man in English. He reached out an arm to steady Kat.

"Thank you, sir," said Kat. She smiled and curtsied. As she did so, she peeked at the headline. Still smiling, she walked off.

"We're in Egypt!" she whispered when she rejoined Jessie. "And it's 1892! We've gone back more than 100 years!"

Kat couldn't contain herself. She twirled in excitement— and bumped into a worker carrying a barrel.

"Many pardons," the man muttered.

"It was my fault," responded Kat.

As the man went on his way, Kat turned to Jessie. "That certainly wasn't English he spoke—or that I did. Was it...?"

"Arabic?" Jessie finished. "It must be."

"I wish I could figure out how the machine does that," Kat sighed. "I mean how it lets us understand other languages. It's sure a lot easier than studying a foreign language in school!"

"There's only one problem," said Jessie. "You won't remember a bit of Arabic when we get back to our own time."

By now she and Kat had passed the tour boat. Farther down the bank was a long flat-bottomed boat. A few workers were loading more crates and barrels aboard.

"Look at that barge," Jessie pointed out. "It's so full it barely floats!"

"I wonder what all those supplies are for?" said Kat. She and Jessie made their way to one of the workers. Speaking again in Arabic, Kat asked, "Where is this boat going?"

"To the place where we are digging, miss," answered the worker. "To the excavation site at Amarna."

Excavation site! Kat was so excited that she forgot to reply. But Jessie said, "Amarna? Well, thank you for your help."

At that, a tall bearded man who was passing by halted. "You speak Arabic," he said in a strong British accent. "And you are headed for Amarna? Thank goodness, you have arrived at last! And just in time!"

He snatched the traveling bag from Jessie's hand. "Let me carry this for you," the stranger said. Bag in hand, he marched toward the barge. Halfway up the ramp, he called back to them. "Please hurry!" he ordered. "We are about to leave!"

For a second, Jessie stood frozen, staring after the man. Then she grabbed Kat's elbow and started forward. "Come on! We have to follow him! He's got the time machine!"

STARDUST CLASSICS titles are written under pseudonyms. Authors work closely with Margaret Hall, executive editor of Just Pretend.

Ms. Hall has devoted her professional career to working with and for children. She has a B.S. and an M.S. in education from the State University of New York at Geneseo. For many years, she taught as a classroom and remedial reading teacher for students from preschool through upper elementary. Ms. Hall has also served as an editor with an educational publisher and as a consultant for the Iowa State Department of Education. She has a long history as a freelance writer for the school market, authoring several children's books as well as numerous teacher resources.

NICK BACKES, illustrator of *Alissa and the Dungeons of Grimrock*, began his career as a freelance illustrator in San Francisco in 1980. He has always been interested in art and credits his teachers for helping him develop this interest.

In addition to his work as an illustrator, Mr. Backes enjoys designing sets for local theater productions and has done work with children's theater.

Nick Backes lives in Oklahoma City, Oklahoma. He shares his home with Pete, a female kitten. He admits that he didn't know Pete was a girl when he named her.

PATRICK FARICY, the cover illustrator, was born and raised in Minnesota. He began his art education there, studying communication design, illustration, and fine art at the School of Associated Arts in St. Paul. He completed his studies at the Art Center College of Design in Pasadena, California.

Since graduating in 1991, Mr. Faricy has been living in California and working as a freelance illustrator. His clients include Coca-Cola, Kellogg's, Busch Gardens, and Warner Brothers.

When he's not painting, Patrick Faricy spends his time writing and playing music, going to the movies, and talking with friends. And he is always on the lookout for something new and different to add to his frog collection!